LOGAN

IN

OVERTIME

Other books by Paul Quarrington:

The Service
The Life of Hope
Home Game
King Leary
Whale Music

*Winner of the 1988 Stephen Leacock
Award For Humour*

LOGAN
IN
OVERTIME

Paul Quarrington

Doubleday Canada Limited, Toronto

Canadian Cataloguing in Publication Data

Quarrington, Paul
    Logan in overtime

ISBN 0-385-25152-1

I. Title.

PS8583.U33L6 1990   C813'.54   C89-095362-7
PR9199.3.Q37L6 1990

Jacket design: Ross Mah Design Associates
Illustration: Franklin Hammond
Typesetting: Southam Business Information
    and Communications Group Inc.
Printed and bound in the U.S.A.

Published in Canada by
    Doubleday Canada Limited
    105 Bond Street
    Toronto, Ontario
    M5B 1Y3

This one is for a rainy day at the Lodge.

"Let's pretend," a voice suggested, "that we're one of those Frank Capra movies."

"How do we do that?"

"You know. Here we are, up in the heavens, looking down."

"Right. And all you see on the screen is a bunch of nebulae and assorted twinklies."

"Exactly."

"With violins," another voice suggested.

"Do they like this sort of stuff?"

"Some do, some don't."

"Okay. Here we go. Look down. Look away down there. Look at the town of Falconbridge, Ontario, population, thirteen thousand."

"Thirteen thousand and one if we count him."

"There he is. Staring right back at us, coincidentally."

"Is it he with whom we are going to fuck around?"

"Well," came a voice, considering, "he's doing a pretty crackerjack job of fucking around with himself. We're going to help him."

"What's he got? Marital problems? Financial difficulties? Mental anguishes? Emotional instability? Physical abnormalities and/or diseases?"

"He's got all sorts of general problems. We're here for something specific."

"Like what, for instance?"

"You guys ever hear of a game called hockey?"

DAY ONE

One

L ogan looked for constellations.

He was grateful that the winter's night fell early, because it gave him this to do in the long hour he had to waste.

Once, as a small child, he had entered his father's library. (This was long, long ago, when Logan's father was a well-respected small-town doctor. His father was no longer well respected, nor even a small-town doctor.) Little Logan had pulled a huge book from the shelf, a book with the magical word ASTRONOMY creeping along its spine. Logan had to lay the volume on the floor and pull it open with both hands. He was amazed and delighted at the things in the sky—the crab, the bull, the hunter and his dog.

Logan had ever since been unable to find these things. He'd spent hours with his eyes pointed at the stars, searching for greater and lesser gods, but so far he'd come up empty-handed.

Logan folded his arms and tried to think of other ways to waste the hour.

The hour occurred every other Friday. Home games. Logan left work at six o'clock, the puck was dropped at eight, the Falcons weren't even allowed in the Coliseum until an hour before face-off.

So Logan was left with this hour. He wished, more than

3

anything else, that he could spend it at the Dove Hotel. That was out of the question.

He'd tried it once. Logan entered the Dove furtively to sit himself down at one of the little round tables, thinking that was somehow more sedate than climbing aboard a stool at the long bar. Logan even brought a newspaper with him, the *Morning Star*, and he made crisp folds that left a quarter page framed for reading. LOGAN LETS IN SOFT ONE, read the headline.

June the barmaid approached. She looked confused and harried. June did not seem equipped to deal with the world, a fact that routinely twisted Logan's heart.

Logan ordered *one* small bottle of ale.

Logan almost blurted out "The usual!" because that was how June wanted the world. But Logan had resolve. One bottle. Furthermore, he instructed June that he under no circumstances could have more than the one.

June smiled sadly and made for the fridges. Along the way townspeople waved their hands, but June ignored them all, hurrying to get this peculiar thing for Logan, this single bottle of beer.

Logan read the newspaper. He felt no connection with the Logan who'd let in a soft one.

The beer came. Logan fished out bills and tossed them on June's tray. She started to make change, pushing around quarters and dimes in a chipped ashtray that nestled among the bottles. "Keep it," said Logan.

June sighed, satisfied that at least one moment had evolved normally.

It took Logan about four minutes to consume the beer, nursing every mouthful miserably.

Logan waved June over and ordered *one* glass of draught beer, making it clear that he under no circumstances could have more than the one.

The draught glass seemed ridiculously small in Logan's huge and horny hand. He tossed the beer down his throat angrily. Logan banged his fist on the table, demanding a quart bottle of

4

Export Ale. By the time he'd finished that, his problem was not how to kill time but how to get as drunk as possible in the few minutes left. That problem was solved routinely: a double tequila and another quart bottle of Ex.

Then Logan wandered over to the Falconbridge Coliseum, vacant and dizzy.

The first three shots got by him. The third was the most insulting, a weak shot taken from the blue line by a skinny kid that no one had ever seen before.

Big George pulled Logan with a little jerk of his thumb, substituting the corpulent Warren Bermondsey. Logan pulled off his cage and made for the dressingroom. He changed without showering and was back at the Dove Hotel in no time.

June stared at him, aghast. "There's a game tonight."

"Nope," said Logan. "Night off." Logan gave June a broad wink. He wasn't yet drunk enough to desire the matronly barmaid, but he allowed as he would be in time. "Bring me a double—"

But June was already gone to fill the standard order, a double tequila and a quart of Ex.

The memory of that night (more accurately, the lack of memory of that night) pulled hard at something inside Logan. He would avoid the Dove at all costs.

Instead, Logan wandered the streets of Falconbridge, Ontario, and looked, without success, for constellations.

∞   ∞   ∞

The following people were at the Dove Hotel: Jay Fineweather, Jean-Guy Cabot and Elmore Daisy.

Elmore Daisy sat in a corner drinking chartreuse. He was the only person in the town who drank chartreuse, and he drank it infrequently, but the Dove Hotel kept it stocked, yellow and green, three or four bottles with the whiskey and rum.

While still a very young man, Elmore had opened a number

of used appliance dealerships throughout southern Ontario, cunningly naming them Daisychains. He arrived in Falconbridge and bought things. Daisy bought the newspaper, the radio station and the local CBC affiliate. He also produced and syndicated "The Buck Tanager Adventure Hour." Elmore Daisy *was*, in fact, Buck Tanager, disguised in a glittery suit and sparkly Stetson. On his weekly show he ran very long films of these "adventures." Not much happened; little forest animals got blasted to smithereens and little fishes were hauled into boats and clubbed with paddles. This show was a huge success, not so much in Canada or even Ontario as in places like Japan and South Africa.

Elmore was also a great hockey enthusiast, so he bought a team and installed it in the obscure Ontario Professional Hockey League. The OPHL had seven teams, all owned by men who had become wealthy in the same small area of southern Ontario. It was professional because these men made a big show of paying the boys for the benefit of the tax people. They certainly didn't pay them much, and all but the thriftiest had to find casual employment. Logan was one of the few to have a full-time job (salesclerk at Li's Hardware), but then, he had more bad habits.

Elmore/Buck was hatching a plot. As owner and general manager of the Falcons, Daisy had been offered the goaltending services of a young man named Henri Gauguin, who had an excellent reputation. Logan, of course, had no such reputation. Elmore Daisy was trying to figure out a way of getting rid of Logan, which, for reasons of his own, he found problematic.

At a table some distance removed sat Jay Fineweather and Jean-Guy Cabot, Logan's teammates. Jay was nursing a single bottle of beer, a trick that amazed Logan. Jay even pulled off this stunt *after* some games, drinking a lone ale and then heading home. Jean-Guy was having a 7-Up and relating a story about Logan. It seems that the previous night, Logan had been spotted standing in the middle of Round River (which luckily was frozen tight, although Logan was probably too drunk to notice) and singing. He was singing and, according to Jean-Guy, blubbering like a baby.

Jean-Guy laughed, but Jay Fineweather didn't. Jay scowled and put out his cigarette, grinding down on the butt long after the ember had died. "How did he get home?" Jay demanded.

"Lottie," answered Jean-Guy, laughing again. Lottie Luttor was a large red-headed woman who had a crush on most of the Falconbridge Falcons. "That Logan," said Jean-Guy, "is a guy of hell."

Jay Fineweather nodded.

∞ ∞ ∞

A map of Falconbridge, Ontario, in its most simplified version would be a cross. King Street ran north and south, intersected by Lowell Avenue. The residential streets spiderwebbed around this basic plan with no logic. The whole thing was contained by Round River, an ambitious creek of curious meanderings.

So Logan stood at the corner of King and Lowell (if he turned around he'd be greeted by a handpainted sign, THE DOVE, but Logan was too canny to turn around) and considered another time-wasting option. He would hike down King Street to Birds of a Feather and visit Kristal.

He dismissed the idea almost immediately. Even discounting the danger of drunkenness, Birds of a Feather was a hateful place. Moreover, it was Happy Hour, which Logan found very depressing. The staff and regulars tended to dislike Logan, with the possible exception of Kristal Donahue. They were used to seeing him barge into the club at a quarter to closing and order a massive, encyclopaedic last call. Logan would stand shakily near the white baby grand. Kristal would play her most haunting song, "Try to Remember (the Kind of September)." As soon as she opened her mouth, Logan would go to pieces. Mr. Palermo had even asked Kristal not to play "Try to

Paul Quarrington

Remember" when Logan was around—Logan's crying jags
didn't help business.

*All this reminded Logan to remember Kristal laughing in his bed.
One morning Logan had said something fairly inane, but it had tickled
Kristal's funny bone. Kristal had sat up in bed and laughed with all her
being. The sheets had fallen away and Logan had been wondrously
flabbergasted by the merry bouncings of her breasts. Remembering this
was Logan's favourite activity, next to searching for constellations, and
certainly more fun. Lately, however, the memory was accompanied by a
tiny sadness, a poor country cousin with a cardboard suitcase.*

Logan felt sad, now, thinking about Kristal Donahue. That
made him want to go to Birds of a Feather even more, not to see
her but Koko. Koko was, in Logan's opinion, Logan's only real
friend in the world. Koko was the military cockatoo that Mr.
Palermo bought when he decided (foolishly) to open a piano
bar in a small Ontario town and call it Birds of a Feather. Koko
was enormous and beautiful, violently coloured. His cage
stood beside the piano. Most of the time he would rest on the
perch, mute and unmoving. But Koko seemed to favour some
people, and upon seeing a favourite the bird would begin a
slow, rhythmic bouncing and an unintelligible squawking.
Koko seemed to like Logan most of all. When Logan stumbled
into the bar, Koko would fly from the perch with a splendid
howl.

∞   ∞   ∞

Koko flew from the perch with a splendid howl, and Kristal
Donahue wondered if Logan had come into the bar. As she
wondered, her right hand hit a gruesome chord. The patrons
were used to clankers, certainly, but this was painful in its
dissonance. Kristal smiled apologetically and took a look
around the room. When she didn't see Logan, she was relieved
and disappointed.

Kristal didn't know how she felt about Logan. This was the
subject of her most recent composition, "I Don't Know How I

8

Feel About Him," which was finished except for the bridge and most of the lyrics. Kristal and Logan had become lovers almost as soon as they met, but they had yet to become very good friends. Lately, Logan spent more and more of his time drunkenly baying at the moon.

Kristal hit another weird chord. A drunk looked at her sternly.

On the other hand, Kristal had many fond memories of Logan. One morning, for instance, he climbed out of bed (Logan seemed unable to sleep past seven-thirty, another big mark against him) and wandered nakedly over to his antique television set. Logan turned it on and spun the channel selector, even though he (like everyone else in Falconbridge) got only one station. Logan focussed his hung-over eyes and then grinned broadly. " 'Captain Kangaroo,' " he announced. "My favourite."

Kristal had laughed and Logan turned to watch her do that. His eyes had widened with delight. That was a very good moment, and even resulted in a pretty decent song, "Thank You, Captain Kangaroo."

But now she didn't know how she felt. She was angry with him more often than not. Kristal reacted to Logan in somewhat the same manner as Koko.

∞   ∞   ∞

Wearily, Logan sat down on a bench that someone had placed on King Street for no good reason. He draped his arms over the back and pushed his legs out lazily. He craned his head upwards and searched the night sky for constellations.

There was a shooting star. Some people counted the sight of a shooting star as a good omen, but not Logan. They merely served to make his search for constellations seem more futile, the points of light refusing to stay in place.

Logan had one remaining option: to go home. Of them all, it was the easiest to dismiss, because there was nothing to do

9

there. His television set got exactly one station. From six to seven it showed local news, sponsored by Elmore Daisy's Daisychains. The local news was hosted by a man and a woman. The man was an ugly specimen, buck-toothed, pock-marked, who read the copy aloud with a miraculously gorgeous voice. Logan sometimes suspected that God gave the guy this voice when He was through talking to Moses. This guy (whose name Logan had taken pains to forget, although if pressed he might guess, accurately, that it was King McGee) fancied himself an authority on sports. If there was nothing else for him to talk about, if the town council were not bickering, if no storm had lately scuppered their county, King McGee would spend a couple of minutes deriding the Falcons in general and their goaltender in particular. Logan would then be forced to holler at the snowy screen. "Where did you get that silly name, anyway? Are you crown prince of the geeks? Hey! What did I ever do to you?"

∞   ∞   ∞

Someone did watch King McGee with regularity, a strangely dressed little boy.

Here's how strangely dressed he was. He wore boxer shorts, tiny and monogrammed. His mother had to order them from a store in Toronto. He also wore an undershirt and argyle knee-socks. He had to wear little garters to prevent the stockings from tumbling down his calves.

Worse was yet to come. He wore a complete three-piece suit, vest and watchfob and all, identical to that of his often-absent father, except that the pants ended just below the knee.

The worst: to challenge the angry Ontario snow, he wore Oxfords and galoshes.

His name was Anthony O'Toole, and his IQ hung around with Einstein's. He was best known in academic circles for his work in probability theory, but for the most part Anthony (never called Tony) directed his prodigious intelligence toward hockey.

The reason he watched the local news with regularity (and we see him watching it now, sitting in the easy chair, one pale leg draped over the other, his fingers drumming nervously on the armrests) is that Anthony supplied King McGee with the sports commentary. Every day Anthony handed Mr. McGee a piece of paper with his opinions neatly printed on it. This is what Mr. McGee read, without embellishment, without (suspected Anthony) comprehension. This arrangement was kept secret, of course, so Logan never knew that it was the eleven-year-old Anthony O'Toole who considered him a washed-up, talentless has-been.

King McGee finished reading and the pretty lady came on. Anthony switched the machine off, leapt down from the easy chair. Then he went to put on his galoshes.

Anthony went to the bottom of the staircase and called upwards. "I'm going to the arena now, Mother, to watch the hockey game." Anthony got no response.

∞   ∞   ∞

The pretty lady (switched off by little Anthony) read the weather and social calendar. She also hosted a program called "A Woman's Diary." Her name was Darla Featherstone, and she was for Logan the most beautiful woman on the planet. Her face and colouring evidenced some strange intermingling of bloods, perhaps Chinese, black and Swedish. Her body was almost frighteningly statuesque. One might think that watching Darla Featherstone would be a pleasant way for Logan to waste the hour, but it made him miserable.

It made Logan's hard-on happy to watch Darla, but Logan's hard-on was usually having fun while the rest of him suffered. Logan's stomach, for example, was routinely upset, especially before a game. Mind you, Logan's stomach was rarely given real food to work with. Logan's brain had the most problems. Even when filled with alcohol, it hurt. Logan's brain was usually confused and occupied itself with things sad and faraway. As for Logan's heart, it was not convinced that the measures Logan was taking (excessive indulgence in alcohol, fruitless searching for constellations, slightly perverse sexual acts with the wrong people) would help much. You see, Logan's heart had a hole in it, about the size of a hockey puck.

Logan took a peek over his shoulder, and there it was, a crude rendering of a dove. Whoever painted the sign had only the vaguest notion of what a dove looked like. This dove seemed mean-spirited and graceless. Logan was not at all surprised to see the sign. If he became confused or lost in thought (an almost perpetual state) his legs would quickly smuggle him over to the Dove.

The situation had changed slightly, in that time had, however haltingly, marched on. It was unlikely he'd have time for more than one beer. Logan leapt through the front entrance before that optimistic thought had a chance to vaporize.

Jay Fineweather and Jean-Guy Cabot, leaving through the same door, pushed Logan back onto the street.

"Hello, journey guy," said Cabot. "Let's find the dungbrains and vanquish them."

"You about ready for a bite of the doughnut, big guy?" asked Jay.

Logan recognized that as hockey banter. *A bite of the doughnut*, a shut-out. Logan didn't respond—mostly he was preoccupied with a re-entry of the Dove.

"Come on, let's go over to the Coliseum." Jay swung his arm around Logan's shoulders and led him as one leads the halt and the lame.

"It's too early, we can't get in," said Logan, working hard to make the tone conversational. He was right, or close to it. Until seven on the nose the dressingrooms were occupied by the Falconbridge Female Falcons, a ringette team of national renown. The hockey players were wary of arriving too early.

"Let's go back to the Dove and I'll buy you guys a brewski."

"Oaken doggies," said Jean-Guy, for which he received a very dark look from Jay.

"It's almost time," said Jay, and then he changed the subject quickly. "Logan, my uncle told me to tell you something. He said to tell you *yahoo*."

"Yahoo," mumbled Logan savagely. Logan took two quick steps forward so that Jay Fineweather was no longer touching him.

The three men walked toward the small-town arena.

Along the way, Logan desperately looked for constellations.

Two

Logan liked away games, mostly because he didn't have to waste an hour after work. He could simply leave Old Man Li's store, climb aboard the team bus, and that was that. The vehicle was a standard yellow school bus, left the standard yellow by Elmore Daisy to complement the DAISYCHAIN USED APPLIANCES painted on it. The bus also announced, in much smaller letters, THE FALCONBRIDGE FALCONS. It was widely rumoured that the team had come within an inch of being THE FALCONBRIDGE DAISIES. It made the players shudder.

The other teams in the Ontario Professional Hockey League were:

The Lewiston Bruins
The Clipperton Cougars
The Hope Blazers
The Westerbury Warriors
The Gormsley Maple Leafs
The South Grouse Bullets

The worst team — not only in the OPHL but anywhere in the world, according to Guinness — was the South Grouse Bullets, winless in four years. It was fitting that South Grouse should produce such a team. South Grouse was a weird little town. (If we take this Marshall Instant Pudding coin, this one that

14

has Logan's profile embossed upon it, and flip it over, look what we see: *Birthplace*, it reads, *South Grouse, Ontario*.)

The best teams were the Lewiston Bruins and the Clipperton Cougars. Bump Strickland played for the Clipperton Cougars before he went to play for Toronto, as many fans will tell you. The OPHL championship (which took the form of the Peddersen Cup, although nobody knows who Peddersen might have been) was traditionally fought between Clipperton and Lewiston.

The remaining four teams were grouped very closely in the middle of the pack, the standings shifting week to week.

The game that week in Falconbridge was against the Hope Blazers, currently tied for third with the Falcons. For the players it was a fairly important game.

Nobody else gave it much thought.

∞   ∞   ∞

They were, for the most part, big boys. They had some small talent and less ambition, and it made sense for them to spend a year or two playing hockey and working part-time for the smelting plant. These players had pretty cushy jobs at Presbo, Inc., directing the other workers, recording figures on long sheets of paper.

There were a few exceptions to this norm. Jay Fineweather, for one. He was a bit older, much more talented, he worked hard at being a farmer. Jean-Guy Cabot was older still, had spent twelve years in the Montreal Canadiens' farm system. Jean-Guy seemed to have no conception of life without hockey. And of course there was Logan. Logan had been a Marshall Instant Pudding coin.

Logan, by the way, is currently naked, so it's time to introduce his knees.

Jay Fineweather, standing beside Logan in the dressingroom, took a quick look. Jay didn't like to look at Logan's knees, but sometimes he couldn't help himself.

15

There was nothing even remotely knee-like about Logan's knees. They were a mass of scar tissue that looked like nothing on earth.

Once, sitting in the Dove Hotel, Jay Fineweather had used that phrase. "Logan," Jay said, "your knees look like nothing on earth."

Logan nodded emphatically. When Logan was drunk his hair became anarchic. His chin grew stubble and his eyes turned red. "Absolutely correct. And, and, you know why, Jay? Because my knees *are* nothing on earth." Logan wrapped his thick fingers around Jay's shirt collar and pulled him closer. Logan had taken his teeth out—another indication that he was pissed as a newt—and the words issued forth soggily. "Some time ago," Logan confided, "my knees were invaded and taken over by mindfuckers from the Dogstar Sirius."

"Oh, yeah," said Jay.

"You see," Logan went on, "on the Dogstar, they don't have bodies. So when they want to fuck around on earth—and they do, all the time—they occupy things." Logan whacked at his left knee sharply and giggled. "They're manky little shitheads to boot."

Jay let a silence drift by. "What the hell happened to your knees anyway?"

"I told you." Logan raised his hand and snapped his fingers, ordering more drinks from June. Logan's fingers were bent, and they banged against each other silently. "Mindfuckers from the Dogstar Sirius."

∞   ∞   ∞

There was only one man in Falconbridge who was likely to endorse, or even fully understand, this theory of Logan's. He was currently marching toward the Coliseum, his arms full of books, his mind brimming with strange ideas and notions.

This was Coach George Tyack, whom you might well have heard of. Tyack had a long and fairly distinguished career as a professional hockey player. The highlights include two Stanley Cup championships, the first won when George Tyack scored in overtime of the final game. Big George was a defenceman, known mostly for his fearlessness when it came to diving in front of pucks speeding toward his team's net. George Tyack would stoically take pucks on the shins, chest and (more than was statistically likely) on the head. His career lasted seven years, during which Big George stopped a couple of hundred shots with his head.

You might think this would alter George's intellect, but the hockey pucks bounced off his head without much damage there. What seemed to have suffered was Big George's capacity for disbelief.

Coach Tyack had an incredible library in his little bungalow, more than three thousand books. *Telekinesis in Professional Sports, Augury by Entrail, Great Religious Thinkers & Their Women, You Are What You Regurgitate*. Fascinating stuff, especially for a gnarly fellow like Logan. Logan's favourite book (he borrowed it and never gave it back) was *The Dogstar*, by Percy St.J. Quodmon.

George Tyack read his books with the seriousness of a Talmudic scholar. The coach was quick to utilize ideas, which meant that the Falcons had undergone several indignities, the worst of which was Coach forcing them to form a human pyramid at centre ice before the commencement of one particular away game.

It might be mentioned that George Tyack, during his career as a professional hockey player, had killed a man. At least, he had caused a man to die. The instrument of death was a bodycheck, perfectly legal. No penalty was assessed on the play and the game-film exonerated Big George. Still, that one incident was remembered with far more clarity by many more people than the goal that won the Stanley Cup.

∞   ∞   ∞

The coach walked into the dressingroom. Logan immediately noticed the luminous aspect to his eyes, which meant that Big George had been reading again.

"Logan!" Big George demanded. "What did you have for breakfast?"

Logan hadn't had anything for breakfast. Logan thought that whoever invented breakfast was an evil man. But, hoping to make his coach happy, Logan lied effusively, "Eggs."

"Oh, shit." George Tyack walked glumly into his office.

∞ ∞ ∞

Logan's back was slapped with much force. Only his reflexes – dulled over time by liquor but still sharp – saved him. He reached forward and grabbed on to his locker an instant before his head would have been wedged in the frame. "Hello, Warren," said Logan.

"Hello, Mr. Logan!" Warren Bermondsey was seventeen years of age and remarkably stout. The few times he'd replaced Logan, Warren had stopped most of the shots seemingly without moving a muscle.

Warren Bermondsey was related to Elmore Daisy, being the son of Elmore's sister Heloise. Warren idolized Logan. Recently he'd given up combing his hair, brushing his teeth and shaving, all in imitation of his hero. Warren had also fittingly taken to drinking too much, which wasn't helping his weight any.

Elmore Daisy, coincidentally, entered the dressingroom at that moment, disguised as his alter ego, Buck Tanager. Elmore Daisy favoured sombre two-piece suits, but Buck Tanager was a flamboyant fashion horse who ordered his clothes from Nudie's of Hollywood. Elmore/Buck almost blinded his players with the sudden display of rhinestones and mirror. The man wore snakeskin boots and his string tie was capped with a rattler skull. The outfit was completed by an enormous ill-fitting white Stetson covering most of Elmore/Buck's face.

The Falcon's owner pulled off the hat and grinned broadly. He cleared his throat and began his traditional pregame pep talk. "Well, pardners . . ."

Logan slipped into Big George's office.

George Tyack was kneeling on the ground and shaking something over his head in a frenzied way. Anyone else would have thought he was playing a spirited game of solitaire craps, but Logan knew better. George Tyack threw three coins on the carpet and translated the results onto a piece of paper. So far he had this:

Big George stole a disdainful glance at Logan. "Eggs," he muttered, disgusted. "For *breakfast?*" Big George waved the coins over his head once more.

"That's what I came to tell you," said Logan. "I didn't eat any eggs. Christ, I wouldn't eat a damn egg if I was starving to death."

Big George threw the coins, noted the results. The coins he used were golden and ancient. One side pictured a strange creature, half-bird, half-human. On the other side was a woman. "You're just saying that to make me feel better," judged the coach, gathering up his coins.

Logan shrugged and wandered over to the coach's desk. He found a book there called *Synchronicity: A Primer*. Logan pulled it open and read about the astounding frequency with which the number twenty-three occurs in the universe.

"Twenty-three," announced Big George, consulting a leather-bound volume. His piece of paper showed this completed hexagram:

19

" 'Po,' " Big George read, " 'is the symbol of falling or causing to fall, and may be applied to the process of decay.' " The coach dished out another black look at Logan, as if this was all his fault.

"Last time I ate an egg," Logan remembered, "must have been twelve years ago."

"Logan, can you keep a secret?" Big George demanded.

"Yo."

"Okay. Then let me just tell you this. There is something very weird going on around here."

"Uh-yeah."

"Very weird. The only thing we got going for us is—" The coach wrinkled his nose and sniffed, which made him grin merrily. "The very air is *excrescential.*"

Logan saw just how weird things were when the door to Big George's inner sanctum opened and Elmore Daisy/Buck Tanager marched in. "Howdy, Logan-boy, you ol' cow-pup!" said Buck Tanager. "I been wantin' to have a little jaw with y'all."

"Howdy!" replied Logan. "Buck, you horse's asshole, how the hell you been?"

"Hey, George, ol' buddy, how's be you let me an' ol' Logan here have ourselves a little tongue-wag, *manno a manno?*"

Big George shot them both a strange look and walked into the dressingroom.

"Okay, Logan," said Buck in his normal, Elmore Daisy voice, which was strident and nasally and made flesh crawl. "Guess to whom I was speaking today?"

"To whom?" Logan was trying to think of other examples of synchronicity involving the number twenty-three. He was pretty certain, for example, that twenty-three was Elmore Daisy's IQ.

"Ed Statler," Elmore said. Ed Statler lived in South Grouse, ran a clothing store and controlled the losingest team in professional sports. "He thinks the world of you," Elmore went on. "Myself, I am sick and tired of you. You are a drunken reprobate. God gave you talent, which you have squandered. If Ed Statler wants you in South Grouse, then that's where you should be."

"Buck—Daisy—" said Logan. "You know I can't go to South Grouse."

"This is your last chance. You win tonight and maybe I'll let you stay."

"But what about—"

"If you lose, Logan, you join all the other loonies and losers down in South Grouse."

"You can't do that. You promised—"

Daisy/Tanager cut him short. "If you lose, you're gone."

"Yeah, well," muttered Logan, "I don't see how I can lose, what with the very air being excrescential and all."

"Oh, you'll find a way."

Three

People with a simplistic view of the universe referred to Jay's uncle Joe Fineweather as a drunk. These same people might call the Mona Lisa a picture. It is undeniably true that Joe Fineweather often was drunk. Joe was sometimes so drunk that he had to abandon autolocomotion and climb aboard the nearest flat surface. Before this stage was reached, Joe Fineweather would be red-faced and raging against invisible enemies.

His greatest foe was the weather. When things turned inclement, Joe took it as a personal affront and challenged the gods. Logan and Jay once had to rescue the old man from the top of the radio station (the tallest building in town), where Joe Fineweather had shinnied halfway up the tower in order to shake his fist at a blackened sky.

When sober, Joe tended to stay clear of town. He fished a lot, read books on comparative religion ("To see what all the fuss is about") and painted in watercolours. The townspeople were wilfully unaware of this, very proud of the bad reputation they'd nurtured for Joe. The people who called Joe a drunk would likewise accuse him of heinous crimes, of lechery involving schoolchildren and little animals.

Carl Luttor (Lottie's father) was one of these people. In Carl's scheme of things, Joe Fineweather was a bad man who did bad things. Unfortunately, Carl had worked himself into a position of some power, that is, he regulated admittance to Falcon home games. Carl stood at the entrance of the Coliseum where, for five dollars, he would let people walk by him, through a turnstile, into the arena to watch the hockey game.

Carl refused to take Joe Fineweather's bill.

Joe immediately assumed there was something wrong with the money. He'd never trusted the stuff to begin with. Joe quickly turned the bill underneath the better of his eyes. It seemed all right. There was the pretty lady staring vacantly into space, on the other side a fishing boat. Joe once more presented the five-dollar bill to Carl Luttor.

That man shook his head adamantly.

Joe Fineweather could only assume that Carl was going to let him watch the game without paying. The gesture brought a lump to Joe's throat. He made a mental note to appoint a Protector to someone close to Carl, perhaps his granddaughter, Charlene. Joe Fineweather waved his hands like a prestidigitator, his one concession to show-biz. Then he tried to step past Carl.

"Oh no you don't," said Carl, grabbing Joe by the collar.

It dawned on Joe that Carl didn't want him to see the hockey game, an unnatural occurrence for which there were many possible explanations. It was Joe's experience that the more unnatural an occurrence, the greater the number of reasons for it.

Joe Fineweather pressed the five-dollar bill into Carl's hand, kicked him on the shin and headed for the crowd.

Joe Fineweather had never attended a hockey game before, so the inside of the Coliseum was new and wondrous. It appeared that everyone who lived in Falconbridge had gathered in the big building, which seemed to Joe an excellent idea and one he should have thought of himself. The women were already sitting on the benches, shivering even in their ski jackets. Many had small children beside them or sitting on their laps. The men were gathered on the mezzanine, talking in small clutches, smoking cigarettes, drinking coffee, eating hotdogs.

Joe pushed his way through the men until he was standing behind the glass that enclosed the rink. He was delighted to see that someone had already painted lines on the ice surface. His work wasn't going to be so hard after all.

Joe tugged on the sleeve of the fellow beside him. "Do you know the man Logan?" asked Joe politely.

"Sure," shrugged the man, both a hockey fan and a regular at the Dove Hotel.

"Where does he perform?"

The man thought of a lot of dirty little jokes, but he knew better than to waste them on Joe Fineweather. The man pointed his forefinger toward the nearest net. "He starts off right there. The second period he goes down there." The man pointed the length of the ice at the other net. Joe was considerably alarmed, mostly because he couldn't see that far. He thought that for the second "period" Logan might be relegated to some vaporous netherworld. "And for the third period," the man finished, "he's back again."

"There are three periods?" confirmed Joe.

"Right," nodded the man. "Three periods. Except for if there's *overtime*."

The word made Joe Fineweather gasp. "Overtime?" he repeated.

"Right. Sudden-death overtime."

Joe shook his head sorrowfully. You spend all your life thinking white men are stupid, and then they spring something on you called *sudden-death overtime*.

Joe worked his way around the curved glass until he was as close as possible to the net that Logan would occupy for two of the three periods unless there was . . .

Joe Fineweather shuddered.

Joe couldn't get immediately behind the net, because immediately behind the net was a fat man sitting on a high stool. The fat man Joe recognized as Boyd Boyce (owner of Boyce Motors), although he had never before seen Boyd Boyce wear thick spectacles with yellowing lenses.

"What are you doing sitting up there, Boyd Boyce?" asked Joe, trying to affect an air of nonchalance.

"I'm the goal judge, what did you think?" Boyd Boyce pointed at a red button sunk into the railing before him. "As soon as I see the puck go in the net, I whack that button."

Joe Fineweather sighed happily. They were stupid after all.

∞   ∞   ∞

The Falconbridge Falcons walked down the corridor gravely, and one after another they stepped onto the ice and skated away. Logan stayed, as always, at the back of the line. He claimed this was superstitious ritual, a lie that was bought because Logan had so many superstitious rituals. In fact, some days for Logan were nothing but falling out of the right side of his bed, carefully mismatching his socks, eating two and a half bowls of Shreddies, reading the newspaper back to front, etc. Logan had more than enough to occupy himself until night-time. So the Falcons let Logan stay at the back because it was one of his rituals. Really, though, it was as close as Logan could come to not stepping onto the ice at all. When his turn came, Logan made the move like a paratrooper. He took a large breath of air, screwed his eyes shut and launched himself into the unknown.

The townspeople of Falconbridge erupted into a long and unified booing.

The townspeople of Falconbridge loved their hockey, but they were none too fond of their Falcons.

There were several reasons for this, including the Falcons' failure to win the Peddersen Cup ever, or even to finish in the top half of the seven-team league. In the final analysis, however, the Falcons' greatest failure was in not putting

Falconbridge on the sporting map. All the other towns had contributed players to the National Hockey League, with the result that all the other towns were getting their names on "Hockey Night in Canada." "That goal was scored by Number Four, Jimmy Peabody. He comes from Kingston, and I believe he played for the Lewiston Bruins, didn't he, Don?"

"That's right, Dan. He played up in Lewiston."

"He played for the Lewiston Bruins last year when they won the Pedderson Cup, didn't he, Don?"

"He did, Dan."

Falconbridge had sent no players to the NHL, although there was a rumour that a year or so back Jay Fineweather had been offered a contract by Detroit but turned it down. The closest link Falconbridge had with professional sports was the drunken bum Logan, who had played for six years in the NHL before his errant ways and otherworldly knees ended that career. So, perversely, Logan received the most abuse from the folk of Falconbridge. They not only hurled verbal abuse, they hurled physical objects. One of their favourite stunts (should Logan let in a soft one) was to shower the goaltender with Aspirin and Alka Seltzer tablets for his obviously debilitating hangover. The kids in the crowd were more serious, and Logan at one time joked that he had been the target of everything but the kitchen sink. That joke's career was ended when some enterprising young hoodlum threw a kitchen sink into the back of Logan's net.

∞   ∞   ∞

At the other end of the rink, a strange-looking creature was stepping onto the ice. He was dressed like his teammates, a black jersey with the word HOPE spelled across his chest in letters that looked to be fashioned from fire. He was heavily protected by padding and his hands were hidden in odd and dissimilar gloves. Logan looked almost the same, except that Logan didn't have HOPE written across his chest. Logan had the word FALCONS encircled by what looked to be a daisychain. What made this creature strange-looking was the mask that he wore. Most of it was blood-red. Yellow forks of lightning lashed out from the sides. In between the openings for the creature's two real eyes was pictured a third one, blue and white like an angry sea. Logan didn't have a fancy Fiberglas mask like that guy. He had a crude and simplistic thing that looked like Logan was playing hockey with a birdcage stuck over his head.

Logan had once owned a beautiful mask, a work of art, that transformed his face into a flying eagle. (Logan had given that mask away. He'd given it to a little man, the saddest man Logan had ever seen. The man was not sad without reason. His wife had recently slept with all of the four friends this guy ever had. The sad little man had wandered away with his face transformed into a flying, screaming eagle.)

At the other end of the ice, the strange-looking creature was gazing at Logan and thinking, "Fucking Logan. I hate Logan."

The strange-looking creature pulled off its lightning-slashed, three-eyed mask, and Logan thought, "It's a *kid*."

Jay Fineweather happened to be cruising by, taking his warm-up circles, and Logan caught him by the jersey. "Jay. Look. They got themselves a fucking kid!"

The kid was blond and big-nosed and had the worst case of acne ever. The kid saw Logan and Jay staring at him, so he sneered. He followed this with a tense little head snap designed to jerk the lanky hair out of his eyes. Then the kid wrinkled his nose savagely back and forth, attempting to dislodge a bit of mucus. Next came a very complicated bit of shoulder-jiggling. All this activity had thrown the long blond hair back over his eyes, so he finished with a reprise of the head snap.

Logan was considerably relieved. "It's okay, he's spastic," he informed his friend Jay.

Jay raised his hockey stick and gave Logan a slap across the shinpads.

Logan began his crease preparations, sliding back and forth with a sideways motion to cut down the glare off the ice. Then he took his stick and swept the debris away, and, having nothing better to do, he dropped to his knees and pretended to fill in a hole, tamping down invisible chips in a very workman-like manner.

The linesmen and referee took to the ice. The referee was Kenny Pringle, Logan noted, which was usually a good thing. Pringle was a reasonable and fair-minded guy. His shortcoming was that he was somewhat out of shape, possessed of a perfectly circular potbelly that popped over his trouser tops. Pringle had some trouble keeping up with the plays, and quite a few illegalities were committed while he was huffing and puffing.

Logan dropped to a crouch (which sent out little expeditions of pain from his alien knees to every corner of his body) and began his stretches, first one leg, then the other. He searched the crowd to see if he could pick out Kristal Donahue. She had a couple of hours before the evening entertainment and sometimes she came to watch the first two periods of a Falcon game. Usually, especially lately, she stayed clear. Logan couldn't see her that night, and he tried to remember if he'd done anything the night before that might have ticked her off. It seemed he had done something quite reprehensible, but his tiny flashes of recollection featured a woman of reddish colouring and considerable girth. *That would be Lottie Luttor, the Rooter Tooter*, reasoned Logan. He re-searched the crowd and, sure enough, he found Lottie sitting in the front row. She smiled and waved and (confirming Logan's suspicions) winked slyly.

It occurred to Logan fleetingly that all was not as it should be.

∞　　　∞　　　∞

Kristal Donahue lived in the only apartment building in

Falconbridge, Ontario. It was a four-storey brownstone that sat at the northwest corner of King and Lowell, kitty-corner from the Dove Hotel.

Walking by the Dove Hotel, Kristal wondered once again why Logan was so fond of the place. The one time she'd entered it, dragged in by that man himself, she'd been appalled at what she saw. There was no happiness inside the Dove Hotel, just a small collection of men and women, uniformly gnarled and hopeless. Kristal hadn't noticed such people living in the town, and she hadn't seen any since, but she knew that inside the Dove Hotel men and women were withering away into the sawdust.

Just as she entered her apartment building, Kristal heard a faraway sound, a soft booing from the Coliseum. Her heart sank; Logan must have let in a soft one. Kristal checked her watch and saw that it was just twenty-five past seven. The boo was the traditional game-opening boo directed at Logan. That made Kristal feel better.

Kristal had considered going to the game, because she really was quite a fan. Her father had played in the National Hockey League, Fred "Greyhound" Donahue. The nickname suited him. Fred was lean, angular, and there was some Micmac blood in him that produced a sleek, smooth aspect. However, they called him Greyhound because he kept getting bussed around, traded from team to team like a piece of equipment. He played for every one of the original six teams and then with expansion he'd added four more to his total. By the time Kristal was seventeen she'd lived in ten different cities. And that's not including times her father had been demoted for little stints to the minors. For the last few years of her father's career, the Donahue family didn't bother finding houses or even apartments; they lived in Holiday Inns.

Given all this, you might find it remarkable that Kristal had learnt to play the piano. You probably wouldn't if you could actually hear her play. Even Logan, possessed of a manifestly tin ear, couldn't help wincing at some of her more bizarre

29

wanderings on the keyboard. And, truth be told, her singing wasn't all it could be. She had a pleasant enough voice, but usually was concentrating so hard on her delinquent fingers that she could only intone in a flat, emotionless manner. Kristal also had an unfortunate predilection for forgetting song lyrics. Logan had walked in on quite a few hostile hootenanies, the entire patronage prompting the words for Kristal.

Kristal unlocked 9-B, let herself in. She immediately went for the white apartment-sized piano, mostly because the silence was hard to take. Kristal hit an augmented eleventh chord, not that she meant to. On the piano lay a yellow legal notepad that had this written on the top page:

He's a

The rest of the yellow sheet yawned, waiting. The word Kristal was most tempted to write was *goof*. She was reluctant to do this only because she'd be putting herself in a bad situation rhyme-wise.

Four

The kid's name was Bram Ridout. People started asking each other what the kid's name was about fifteen seconds into the opening period. The Falcons had taken it to Hope with a vengeance, slamming about six shots point-blank at the Blazer net. Bram Ridout looked like a marionette in the hands of an epileptic, collapsing to the ice to stop one shot, shooting up into the air to bounce the puck from his chest, crumpling again. Finally one of the Blazers managed to fish out the puck. He spotted the winger breaking, fed him a pass, and the forward was away, the centre travelling with him. It seemed to Logan that all five of his teammates were still taking shots on the kid, oblivious of the situation—the Hope Blazers had a two on nobody.

"Well, this is just peachy," muttered Logan. It was almost certainly a goal—whichever Blazer player Logan chose to cover would simply pass to the one he ignored. Logan was tempted to sit down in his crease with a great show of disgust. Still, he wasn't about to a let a spastic kid show him up.

The Blazer right winger was carrying the puck, waiting for Logan to commit himself. Logan took a breath of air and launched himself toward the man. After two strides, Logan broke suddenly and started for open ice and there—incredibly—Logan spotted the puck skittering toward the free man. With a golf-style swing of his stick and a maniacal laugh, Logan propelled the rubber forward. And the gods seemed to be Falcon fans, because Jay Fineweather received the puck, stepped over the Hope red line and had a clear shot at the net. Jay took a wrist shot, sent the puck whistling for the net's upper left corner. Bram Ridout caught it in his trapper, returned the puck to the ice nonchalantly. A Hope Blazer scooped it up, led an assault on Logan. The Blazers stormed down the ice and one of their ranks rifled a shot into the air. Logan shot out his own glove hand, snake-like and angry. Logan held the puck, because he dearly wanted a rest, until Kenny Pringle blew the whistle.

Up in the bleachers, Anthony O'Toole was making notations into a notebook.

$$P(E_2/A) = \Sigma_2 \gamma x + \pi^{2/-2}$$

He was interpolating topological information, having to do with the *connectivity* of ice-hockey rinks.

The man beside little Anthony, a man wearing a purple ski jacket, rubbed his hands together and giggled. "Hey!" He nudged little Anthony in the side. "Looks like it might be a good game, eh?"

Anthony O'Toole stared at his page full of markings. There was nothing there to indicate that the game would or would not be good. Anthony explained this to the man, drawing his attention in particular to that section dealing with the bounded planar network, wherein

$$\delta \Sigma_2 + (F_b - A_b) > 0$$

The man said, "Oh."

$$\infty \qquad \infty \qquad \infty$$

Logan assumed his face-off stance and almost immediately received a puck in the face. It threw him backwards; the crossbar connected against his helmet, producing a sound that deafened and confused him. Frantically, Logan searched for the puck lying on the ice about five feet in front of him. Logan dove at the same time as a Blazer stick arrived. Logan got to the puck first, although his landing lacked any athletic dignity. The townspeople booed.

Logan climbed to his feet slowly. He dealt out a few disgusted remarks at his own defencemen, wandered back to his net. At that moment Logan didn't really care whether the game was won or lost, he only cared that it was fought quickly and left him a goodly amount of drinking time.

∞   ∞   ∞

Statistics dutifully recorded by Anthony O'Toole indicated that at the end of one period the score was tied 0-0. The shots on net were fourteen for the Falconbridge Falcons and twelve for the Hope Blazers. The only penalties that had been assessed occurred at 12:35, when Michaud (Falconbridge) and Gregg (Hope) were sent off for roughing, two minutes each.

The man beside Anthony O'Toole nudged him again and pointed at the notebook. "Well, kid?" he demanded. "Is it a good game or what?"

Anthony made a few rapid calculations. Anthony doubted the results and double-checked them. He had never made a mathematical error in his life, but he felt it prudent to double-check.

"Well?"

Anthony cleared his throat. "All I can suggest at this time," he reported, "is that I trust you are well rested."

∞   ∞   ∞

In the Falcons' dressingroom, Logan was on bended knees, his huge hands wrapped together imploringly. "Please score some goals, you guys," he whimpered. "Score some goals and we'll

33

win the game and then we'll go to the Dove and get hammered and I'll take some dog home and everything will be all right. All right?"

Jay Fineweather spoke for the rest of them. "What about the kid?"

Logan turned bitter. "The kid is *lucky*," he snarled. "He's undisciplined. He's *raw*. You can score on him."

George Tyack rubbed his jaw ponderously. "Maybe you guys should move in close on the kid," he said. "You sure don't beat him from a long ways out."

The Falcons moved in close in the second period. They crowded around Bram Ridout and interfered with him constantly, bumping elbows and knocking him down more than once. They chipped at the puck from a foot or two away, trying sneaky little backhands and flickshots.

The kid altered his style completely, standing up until the last possible moment, confidently dealing with everything that came his way. When the going got extremely heavy, Ridout seemed to reach through the fray, snatch the puck out of the air and force a whistle. The Falcon plan, simply put, didn't work. Indeed, it backfired. Falconbridge was assessed four minor penalties (Huculak, 7:45; Michaud, 10:18; Ogilvie, 11:09; Fineweather 17:08).

The penalties to Normand Michaud and Keith Ogilvie ran consecutively for more than a minute; for that minute the Falcons were shy two men. During this minute Logan was glad that he hadn't eaten any food, because he surely would have soiled himself. It seemed there was more than one puck on the ice for that minute, at least two and probably three or four. They came from all angles and elevations, low from one side, high from the other. And Logan's teammates, despite the thinning of the ranks, were in his way, blocking his vision.

Still, Logan didn't let anything get by him. One stop was purest chance, admittedly—he waved his arms in desperation and the puck bounced into and out of his armpit—but the rest he saw at the last second.

So at the end of two periods of play, the score was still tied, 0–0.

∞ ∞ ∞

Kristal Donahue was back at work at Birds of a Feather. She was playing a rather bizarre rendition of "The First Time Ever I Saw Your Face." Kristal was thinking about the first time ever she saw Logan.

She'd arrived in Falconbridge only the week before. Kristal seemed willing to travel anywhere, so her agent offered her lovely Falconbridge, Ontario, and she'd snapped it up. What surprised the agent was the phone call a day or two later. Kristal had been offered a permanent position (prompted by Mr. Palermo's Quixotic determination to get into Kristal's pants). She'd accepted, was busily searching out an apartment. In short, Kristal was a Falconbridger and so she would remain.

So the first time ever she saw Logan, she'd looked up from her keyboard to find two strangers sitting at the piano bar.

One was astoundingly handsome. The man had golden hair that formed tight little curls. His eyes were a very dark shade of blue, flecked with grey. Both the gold and the blue were made even more vivid by the rich bronze of the man's tanned skin.

This astoundingly handsome man was drinking a beer and grinning broadly. He spoke aloud. "I think you're going to like it here."

For a moment Kristal imagined that this handsome man was talking to her. Then she turned to look at his companion. She was not impressed.

The other man had short, stiff, mucky-coloured hair that stuck out from his head at odd angles, as if the hair was trying to get as far away from the brain as it could. The man had about four days' beard covering his face and even this light growth seemed to spring out bizarrely. His eyes were small and brown and bespoke advanced drunkenness, if not out-and-out

35

lunacy. He looked around Birds of a Feather miserably and said, "Let's get out of here, Lindy."

His friend, this Lindy, shook his head. "You know what the doctor said. Normal people. Normal situations. Now, come on, Logey. Enjoy yourself."

The other man gestured around the nightclub and spilled half his beer. "You call this *normal?*"

His friend hushed him sternly. "The lady's trying to play the piano, Logan."

Logan noticed Kristal. "Hey! Do you know how to play 'Try to Remember'?"

Kristal did in fact know that Tom Jones/Harvey Schmidt classic. She stroked a few odd chords and then opened her mouth to sing. "*Try to remember when life was so tender.*"

That's as far as she got.

Logan went to pieces.

Kristal stopped singing, continued the soft piano chords.

"Keep going," Logan demanded, wiping away tears.

"No, that's fine. Thanks," said Lindy.

"Do it!" bellowed Logan.

"*Try to remember when life was so tender,*" sang Kristal gently, "*that dreams were kept beside your pillow.*"

Logan began to sing along in a choked voice, miles off key. "*Try to remember when life was so tender that love was an ember about to billow . . .*"

Lindy grabbed him by the arm. "Let's go, Logey."

Logan sobbed, pulled away, dug his fingernails into the piano desperately.

"*Try to remember,*" sang Kristal to Logan, "*and if you remember, then follow.*"

Lindy managed to drag Logan out of Birds of a Feather. As they left Kristal noticed that Logan walked with a severe limp. That struck her, oddly, as very attractive.

After the set, Vicky the waitress came up excitedly. "Do you know who that *was?*"

"Somebody named Logan," answered Kristal.

"That was Lindy Olver!" shouted Vicky. "Is he gorgeous or what?"

Kristal was distracted and made no answer.

∞   ∞   ∞

At the beginning of the third period, the game was delayed because of a commotion in the crowd. For a moment, a panicked whisper of "Fire!" ran throughout the Coliseum. Several people stampeded for the exits. The fire, though, was under control, managed by Joe Fineweather, who'd also started it. In the area behind Logan's net, Joe Fineweather was burning odd things and creating billows of noxious gas. The old man was doing a dance around it, chanting like a wind on the prairie. No one could get close enough to stop him, so foul was the smell. After a few minutes, Joe Fineweather poured a cup of Coca Cola over his flames ("The only thing this crap is good for," he told anybody within earshot, except nobody was) and the game was resumed.

The smoke wafted slowly over the Plexiglas toward Logan's net. The third period was more than a minute old when it reached the goalie's nostrils. Fortunately, the play was down in the other end, because Logan found himself gagging and dizzy. He reached backwards to support himself on the net's crossbar.

Three Blazers were swarming down the ice, and there was only a lonely Falcon to thwart them. That Falcon, Parker Mackie, tried to take two men out of the play and missed them both.

Logan watched with a detached wonderment as the three men advanced.

To everyone in the stands, the game was as good as over. They groaned. Most of the people pursed their mouths in preparation for the inevitable *boo*.

Logan, though, made the best, if the most unusual, save of his career, throwing himself into the air. No one expected

Logan to launch heavenward, especially the Hope Blazer who chose that moment to rifle the puck. Logan seemed to hover in midair for the moment it took the puck to travel fifteen feet. It bounced off his chest, dropped directly to the ice, at which point Logan fell, covering it.

Joe Fineweather raised his fist over his head and shouted, *"Yahoo!!"* Right then Carl Luttor grabbed Joe and threw him out. Joe Fineweather put up little argument, and the last anyone saw of him that night he was smiling a very self-satisfied smile.

Logan was baffled by his own behaviour and shook his head violently, trying to clear it. He watched the kid Bram Ridout make a series of brilliant saves.

A moment later, Logan's heart began to beat rapidly. He saw Ridout tumble over backwards, ending up sprawled along the ice, his head inside the net. And then Logan watched the puck pop right onto the blade of Vic Pheresford's stick.

Logan screamed "SHOOT!" as loudly as his lungs would allow. He could almost taste the beer and feel a soft bosom.

It was a good shot, a foot off the ice and flying dead-straight over Bram Ridout. Then a form materialized on top of Ridout. It took Logan a split-second to realize it was the kid's glove. It took Logan longer to see that the puck was in the glove's pocket.

Logan bellowed, a raw sound that filled the Coliseum and silenced the people applauding Ridout's miracle. Everyone turned to look. Logan howled, long and anguished. Occasionally he slapped his stick with all his might, but that sound was drowned out as the holler echoed upon itself. Abruptly, Logan fell silent, although his bellow still rang lightly in the rafters.

Everyone stared at Logan, the drunken bum with twisted knees and a matching brain.

Logan assumed his stance.

∞   ∞   ∞

Little Anthony O'Toole, erudite as he was, was able to predict it at 8:07 of the third. He offered a mathematical proof as to its inevitability a minute later.

The idea first occurred to Logan with about five minutes to go, and very nearly reduced him to tears.

The crowd had a pretty fair hunch it was coming, too. As the period drew to a close they became oddly quiet.

And so on the Friday, at about a quarter past ten, the horn sounded.

They were in overtime.

DAY TWO

Part Two

Five

Logan awoke, severely hung over, when a tiny fist landed squarely on his nose. He opened his eyes, alarmed, but closed them again as the tiny fist bounced off his forehead. Logan kept his eyes closed, hoping that this would somehow quiet the tiny fist. He felt a sharp stinging in his left eye and knew it hadn't worked.

"Charlene," he mumbled, "why the hell are you hitting me?"

"To track your tension," came the high-pitched reply, and then Logan felt a tiny-fisted combination, the left connecting with the jaw, the right coming over to meet his crown.

Logan felt movement in the bed beside him. "Heeheehee!" giggled Charlene cruelly. "Look! Mommy's bum!"

Logan rolled over and saw Lottie Luttor's considerable rear end aimed at him. He tried to pull the sheets over it, but Lottie had yanked them tightly around her head.

"It sure is big," muttered Charlene, apparently in awe.

"You don't know the half of it," replied Logan.

"What does that mean?" shrieked Charlene, throwing a right jab into Logan's cheekbone. She was eight years old and took umbrage if someone said something she didn't understand.

"Charlene!" Logan did his best to sound parentally strict. "Don't you have to be in school or something?"

"SCHOOL!?" screamed Charlene. "It's Saturday! You don't go

to school on a Saturday, idiot!" Charlene tried to look calm, but she was inwardly panicking. She was still not quite sure of the limits to a grownup's power. Perhaps they were capable of sending kids to school on a Saturday.

Logan laughed, sensing Charlene's terror. She attacked viciously, tiny fists flying everywhere. Logan managed to catch her wrists and hold on long enough to make her stop. Tears ran down her cheeks.

"What's the matter?"

"*You*," snarled Charlene. She struggled briefly to free her hands but her energy was spent. Logan judged it safe to let go.

"Make my breakfast," Charlene ordered. "Chocolate milk, Froot Loops and a peanut butter and banana and pickle sandwich."

Half-asleep, Logan's stomach misunderstood, thinking it was being called upon to consume all that shit, and sent down a load of bilge for immediate evacuation.

Logan leapt out of bed and headed for the bathroom.

"I can see your bum!" shouted Charlene.

Logan threw the bathroom door shut and sat down heavily. His actual business was conducted almost immediately, but Logan decided to linger. His stomach had been more damaged by Charlene's tears than by her breakfast menu.

Logan ran a memory check on the previous night. His memory was complete and linear only until the game had been stopped. After that it became cloudy for about an hour (it had something to do with a car, driven by Lottie, foolishness of the highest order) and after that it was anybody's guess.

Logan thought about the game. He said, aloud, "Fucking kid."

There came a knocking, a pounding, on the door. "Logan?"

It was Lottie.

"I'm sitting on the john," Logan informed her.

"Well, get the hell off it! What do you think I want to do, powder my nose?"

"Just a second." Logan got up and unlocked the door. Lottie entered, naked and pink, stretching upwards to kiss Logan on the lips.

Lottie Luttor was so enthusiastic about her sexual activities that the locals, slightly abashed, couldn't even accord her a reputation. Lottie was not one, for example, for mysterious explanations about her daughter's existence. "Oh, *gawd*," she'd say, if asked, "it was Smiley Burnett. You know Smiley Burnett? Smiley Burnett and the Happy Valley Boys." Smiley Burnett was a country and western singer who made annual appearances in Falconbridge. Despite his name, and the appellation of his band, Smiley was a dour sort. His songs had to do with suicide, alcoholism, the death of children, head-on collisions on a stormy highway. Charlene had quite a bit of Smiley Burnett in her, always eyeing the world suspiciously, waiting for tragedy to take a big bite.

"Lottie," asked Logan, "were you driving last night?"

"I got to pee so bad I can taste it," responded Lottie, and she sat herself down. "Course I was driving. You were shaking so bad you couldn't hold the wheel. I never saw anythin' like it." Lottie shook her hands to show Logan exactly how badly he had been shaking. Then she clucked her tongue appreciatively. "God, you were great last night."

"So was the fucking kid."

"You're cuter than the kid," said Lottie as she rose and marched about the little room. When she was dressed (Lottie dressed in a kind of uniform, blue jeans and a Falconbridge Falcons sweatshirt) it was easy enough to think Lottie fat. Logan knew there was nothing fat, at least nothing soft or jelly-like, about her. She was tightly packed, glowing crimson pulchritude. Ordinarily it wouldn't require much more than one or two steps (Lottie looked appealing stretched out upon her bed, but in motion Logan found her maddening) but Logan was not to be roused.

45

Lottie crossed over to the bathtub and opened the faucets, letting the water run full force. The sound inside the tiny washroom was very loud. Lottie almost had to shout. "Charlene's watching TV. She won't hear a thing." Lottie arranged two bathmats end to end, and then she lay down on them. After a moment she raised herself on to her elbows and stared at Logan quizzically. "What are you waiting for, an engraved invitation?"

"You're not fooling her, you know," said Logan. "She's a smart kid."

"I get my child-rearing advice from Mr. Spock," replied Lottie testily. "Now get the hell over here."

Logan still hesitated.

"You want to do something different or something?" offered Lottie. She flipped over and raised herself to her hands and knees. She rotated her rear end rather appealingly, but to Logan it was still *Mommy's bum*.

Lottie turned over again, sitting up and crossing her arms sternly. "What? You want to do that *weird* thing?"

Logan shook his head dumbly.

"What's the matter, Logan? Cat got your dick?"

Logan shrugged his shoulders with a great show of exasperation. "The little guy must be tuckered out from all the action last night."

"Logan, you immense fuck-up, we didn't do anything last night."

Logan smiled and shrugged again. This caused a series of stabbing pains to course throughout his brain.

"Come here, Logey," said Lottie quietly. Logan obediently took two steps forward. Lottie reached up to the lip of the tub and took hold of the soap. She ran water from the faucet over it and rubbed until she produced a cloud of lather. She then took the head of Logan's penis into her mouth and stroked the shaft with her soapy hands.

Don't give in, General Logan ordered his privates sternly.

"There we go!" said Lottie about four seconds later.

46

Traitor, thought Logan as he stared at his hard-on.

Lottie lay back down again. "All aboard!" she called out with a cackle.

Logan was striking a bargain with his hard-on. Logan would allow his hard-on this pleasure, and in return Logan's hard-on would let Logan go home and take a nap and not bother him for the rest of the afternoon. Fair enough, both parties agreed. Logan dropped to his knees. Lottie grabbed his head and yanked it down between her legs.

Logan tried to remember exactly where it was he had given away his beautiful soaring-eagle, moulded Fiberglas goalie's mask. If it was in Falconbridge there was a slim chance he could find it, maybe even before five o'clock. He tried to picture the man he had given it to, but could come up only with a shadowy portrait of sadness.

Lottie grabbed Logan by the hair and yanked on him until he lay the length of her. She gave his hard-on a couple of tender pulls by way of toning, guided him into her, and dug her fingers into Logan's backside.

Lottie came almost at once, exploding toward the ceiling. Logan hung on for dear life. After a few moments Lottie settled down. She maintained a gentle pulse and whispered, "Okay, Logan darling. It's fucking *overtime*."

Logan was a bum in the NHL and only slightly better than a bum in junior, but he had this one small accomplishment – he'd never lost a game in overtime. Overtime frightened and enraged Logan, lending him strengths and talents that were never hinted at. Mothers have been known to lift automobiles if a child should be trapped underneath: so it was with Logan in overtime.

The night before, Logan had played well in regulation time, but really no better than a journeyman professional goaler should be expected to play in a semiprofessional league, mathematically cutting down the angles, blocking shots in a calculated, methodical fashion. Logan stayed upright because his knees liked it that way.

47

When overtime came, all that changed. Logan took command of his knees, telling them he didn't care what Dogstar they were from, if he wanted them to buckle they would damn well do so. His knees, confused by the sudden change in temperament, were cowed into submission. Next Logan informed his stomach that puking was not the best way to deal with the sudden influx of fear. Rather, he suggested, convert it into a high-test adrenalin only slightly less potent than Dexedrine. His stomach, eager to do something other than drink and vomit, got to work immediately. His brain was the hardest to tame, but with work Logan kept it centred on the piece of rubber called the puck. And Logan simply refused to let the puck enter the net.

His heart was whole and happy.

That's how it is in overtime. The man starts down at the far end. You watch him coming. The bite of his skateblades is the only sound. His eyes are animal, his legs machine. The whole world holds still as he draws the stick back. He shoots!

"HE SCORES!" shouted Lottie, exploding beneath Logan.

"HE DOES NOT!" shouted Logan. He came hard, his mind blank but for Bram Ridout's third eye.

The water fell over the side of the bathtub.

Logan fell asleep.

∞   ∞   ∞

Later, Lottie puttered around the kitchen in an oversized T-shirt, preparing eggs. Logan drank a cup of black coffee and avoided the recriminating glares of Charlene Luttor. When he was sufficiently caffeine-jacked, Logan made silently for the door. Lottie was whistling over a fry pan, Charlene was face-deep in Froot Loops, Logan judged it best not to disturb anybody, to simply slip out the door and disappear. . . .

"Hey, buddy," said Lottie.

Logan turned around resignedly. But instead of coming

forward to be kissed, Lottie tossed a set of keys through the air.

Logan swiped at them. The keys sailed through his fingers and landed noisily on the floor.

"Geez. I hope you do better than that tonight," said Lottie with a chuckle.

Logan stared at the keys between his feet and hoped the same thing. "What are they for?"

"The car, nimrod," Lottie replied, pointing with her spatula toward the street. "I told Jay you'd have the car back before eleven o'clock. So you got until half an hour ago."

"Why did you borrow Jay's car?" asked Logan, retrieving the keys.

"Why?" Lottie slapped her plate on the table and plunked herself down behind it. She cut a piece of egg with the edge of her fork and tossed it into her mouth. "*I* borrowed it," she said, "because *you* wanted to drive up to the top of Owsley Mountain."

"Right," nodded Logan, pretending to remember. "I like the view of town."

"Town?" Lottie broke the yolk. "You were looking for those things in the sky."

"Constellations?" guessed Logan.

"Correct-a-mundo."

"What's a consolation?" demanded Charlene, staring at Logan.

"Don't ask him," Lottie said. "He's never seen one."

Charlene ignored her mother. "What's a consolation?"

"Charlene," responded Logan a little urgently, "there are things in the sky. There's a big hunter, and a dog, and a unicorn and a bull. All sorts of things, right up there in the sky."

"Where?" asked Charlene, disbelief pulling at the edges of her mouth, something else lighting her eyes.

"Well . . . ," said Logan, biting at his lip. "They're a little tricky to find."

Charlene nodded and returned her attention to her breakfast.

Logan turned and headed for the door.

"Logan?" said Charlene quietly.

"Yeah?"

"I hate you."

"Yeah." Logan left.

Six

Logan residue, Kristal thought bitterly.

Logan, his nerves jangling, would leap out of bed around eight o'clock, even earlier. He would stand in the middle of the room, naked and disoriented. Kristal's system didn't kick in until noon, but her brief association with Logan had whacked it all out of kilter, and now it was eight o'clock in the morning and Kristal Donahue was standing in the middle of the room, naked and disoriented.

She hadn't gone to sleep until five. She'd come into her apartment, restless after her night at the club, and switched on the television. Kristal, like everyone else in Falconbridge, got exactly one station. Elmore Daisy had steadfastly forbidden the cable companies to approach Falconbridge, savouring his small-minded monopoly. Some disgruntled citizens had forked over thousands for satellite dishes, only to find them useless. There was some speculation that Elmore Daisy had contrived to launch his own interference sputnik. So Kristal turned on her set, settled into her easy chair – a huge reclinable monster, equipped with an inner mechanism that made it vibrate – and watched whatever Elmore offered. At two o'clock in the morning, Elmore's station showed old movies that Elmore didn't have to pay for. It showed kung-fu movies subtitled in Hungarian. It showed filthy movies, where people walked around naked and spoke in a tongue that Kristal could

51

not recognize. It showed grade-B science-fiction movies, Kristal's favourite.

The commercials were particularly diverting. Advertising time went mighty cheap that time of night, maybe a nickel a minute, and was snapped up by exterminators and cesspool cleaners. Some remained unsold, so Elmore Daisy put on spots for his own shows. There was an ad for the "Buck Tanager Adventure Hour" ("We gone out in the bush with my ol' buddy King McGee this Saturday, folks!") and for "A Woman's Diary." The host of "A Woman's Diary" was a gorgeous creature named Dharma Fenster or some such silliness. She sat with her legs crossed and stared blackly into the camera. "This week on 'A Woman's Diary,' " she said – she had a very silly voice, Kristal noted – "I begin a special investigation into the world of *men*."

"I'll be sure to watch, cutie-pie." Five o'clock in the morning and Kristal was making snide remarks to the television set. She got up wearily, went to bed, and it seemed like scant minutes later that she was standing in the middle of the room, naked and disoriented.

Kristal wandered into the kitchen to get a glass of milk. More Logan residue. Logan drank almost as much milk as beer and tequila, Kristal's fridge was loaded with the stuff. Kristal marched along sleepily, yawning, scratching her butt. She poured milk into a huge tumbler and sipped. As she did, she noticed the huge silver bird-whistle.

She'd purchased it from a man at Birds of a Feather. A bird-whistle salesman, in point of fact. The club was frequented by salesmen, mostly because salesmen were always lying to each other, claiming to have scored while visiting Birds of a Feather. No one ever got lucky at Birds of a Feather. No one got lucky, no one was happy during Happy Hour, but the place was always packed, especially on Friday nights. This salesman had come in, flushed and excited from the hockey game. "It's not even over!" he told the people clustered around the piano. "Is that goalie ever good!"

"Logan?" asked Kristal quietly.

"No, the kid. Not Logan. Logan's a bum."

The people at the piano had nodded glumly.

After a couple of drinks the man had his bird-whistles out of their carrying case. He distributed them amongst the patrons, and Kristal's last set was accompanied by chirrups, trills, twitters and warbles. Kristal was fascinated by the biggest of the whistles, which was about a foot long. She wondered what sort of bird it was meant to attract and, in a moment of, well, in a very strange moment, she'd forked over cash.

Kristal picked the whistle up. She marched over to the kitchen window and banged it open. The winter bolted in like a cat that had been left outside all night long, rendering the naked Kristal bluish and bumpy. She raised the whistle to her lips, stuck the sounding-end out into the world and tooted with all her might.

Nothing.

Kristal went back to the livingroom, climbed into her easy chair, pulled a blanket over herself. She powered on the television set—her machine was equipped with remote control, a useless convenience in Elmore/Buckville—and settled back.

Captain Kangaroo was talking to Grandfather Clock.

Kristal went to sleep.

∞   ∞   ∞

Logan drove slowly in deference to Jay Fineweather's old car. It was an enormous and unsightly motoring sedan, a land-shark, which some of the townspeople still referred to as the "Wagonburner Wagon." This isn't really an indication of the local people's innate bigotry—the name was actually thought up by Jay himself, and he'd written it across the automobile's wide finny back with stencil and spraypaint. Jay Fineweather had also outfitted the car with a bumper sticker (CUSTER DIED FOR YOUR SINS), and he'd fashioned a large feather, as from a war bonnet, to replace the car's original hood ornament. Years ago (so Logan had been told) the car had struck terror into the hearts of the citizenry. It came swooping out of the hills, filled to overflowing with Jay and his buddies. The car sped along Falconbridge's streets and dirt roads, screeching tires at every opportunity. Empty beer bottles flew from the windows with incredible regularity, as if ale fuelled the car's savage prowling.

The car was now as sedate as Jay Fineweather himself. There were still some signs of its errant ways (dents running the length of the side, the vinyl seatcovers stained and rubbed shiny, some faint ghostly printing on the back, W O R E ON), but the automobile now refused to go faster than a leisurely crawl. Such a speed was good enough for Logan. It was a rare and beautiful winter's day, cold but cloudless, the blue of the sky stretched around the earth from rim to rim. Logan put on his sunglasses (mirrored to hide his eyes) and rolled down the window. Despite the cold, the sun soon warmed him comfortably.

Jay Fineweather lived outside the town on a small tract of land that his father, Edgar, had bought near the end of his days. Edgar Fineweather had spent a lifetime on the reserve dreaming of owning farmland. He finally achieved this ambition and lived on the property with his wife, two sons and brother Joe. Eight months after he took possession, Edgar tried to pull some logs up a sharp incline with a tractor. Jay's father was uncertain about many aspects of farming, about this one disastrously so. The tractor flipped over backwards, crushing Edgar Fineweather. Joe and Jay Fineweather decided to work the land together, the younger son, Tommy, being still a toddler. A year later, Jay's mother, Mary, put a load of laundry into the machine. The cantankerous washer bolted forward, breaking her toes. With her foot in a thick cast, a tumble down a flight of stairs broke her hip. In hospital she contracted pneumonia and then complications, and died, barely into her forties. Finally, little Tommy, dissatisfied with whatever was showing on their huge antique television (it was "Captain Kangaroo"), went to turn the channel. The machine tumbled from its stand, and Joe and Jay Fineweather were all alone. Jay got his Wagonburner Wagon, Joe got himself pickled, the farmland lay barren and useless.

Two summers back, Jay Fineweather had returned to the land. Jay worked incredibly hard, first because he couldn't afford outside help, secondly because he distrusted and therefore never used machines.

∞   ∞   ∞

The Fineweather land was enclosed by a split-rail fence. Signs hung everywhere: PRIVATE PROPERTY. NO HUNTING OR FISHING. Logan turned up the small road marked by the J. & J. Fineweather mailbox. The road was treacherous and icy, but the ex-Wagonburner Wagon, now matronly and quiet, drove up to the farmhouse surely.

Logan found both Fineweathers outside, effecting a repair job to an outside window. He caught them in the middle of a shared joke, laughing loudly. Jay Fineweather said, "Ho there, journeyman!"

Joe said, "Greetings, Logan. Greetings, Yahoo."

Logan had been called worse than a yahoo before, although never by Joe Fineweather. He dismissed the odd remark.

"Look, Uncle Joe," said Jay. "We got us a man sapped of energy. He's obviously spent the night with the Rooter Tooter."

Joe Fineweather looked at Logan with a long grin. Actually, his mismatched eyes seemed to focus on some point just above Logan's right shoulder.

Logan tried to change the subject quickly. "Fixing a window, eh?"

Jay Fineweather shrugged, waving a small container of window putty. "Actually, it's preventive maintenance," he explained. "Big storm coming."

55

Paul Quarrington

Logan started to say, "Darla never said anything about it," in reference to the perfect weather/social calendar woman, Darla Featherstone, but instead he said, "I never heard about it."

"Don't you listen, Logan?" challenged Uncle Joe.

"This isn't your officially forecasted storm," admitted Jay.

"The bimbo on the television knows nothing about it," nodded Joe Fineweather. "Have you seen her, Logan? She uses maps!" Uncle Joe laughed derisively. "Maps to tell the weather." Joe cocked an eye at a point above Logan's right shoulder. "But don't worry."

"You know what I need?" demanded Logan suddenly. "A drink."

"You know what you ain't about to get?" responded Jay. "A drink."

Joe wagged a stern forefinger. "Yahoo doesn't like drinking."

"You wanna bet?" snapped Logan.

Joe Fineweather giggled.

Joe spoke seriously. "You can't have a drink, buddy. We got to be at the Coliseum at five."

The Coliseum had been booked for the day by various small-town teams and pleasure-skaters. Some had been willing to relinquish their time, given the extraordinary circumstances. The Falcons and the Blazers were scheduled to play between five-thirty and eight o'clock.

"Just one goal," said Logan. "That's all you guys got to do. Just put one little measly puck past that ugly kid, and then we can get stinko!" Logan winced. *Stinko* was the word Kristal used to describe Logan at his most drunken.

Jay Fineweather clucked his tongue. "I don't know, Logey. The kid was pretty amazing. Both you guys were pretty goddamn amazing. Four fucking overtime periods. Do you have any idea what the shot totals must be?"

The game had gone on until two-thirty in the morning, at which point Kenny Pringle had called both team captains for

56

consultation. "Guys," said Pringle wearily, "I gotta be up in the morning."

"So is it a tie or what?" asked the Blazer captain.

Kenny Pringle shook his head. "In the OPHL, there aren't no ties. It's in the league rules."

Jay Fineweather suggested, "How about a shoot-out?"

Pringle shook his head. "Nope. What the rule book says is the only thing we can do is recess the game. Stop for now, and then start up again tomorrow or something."

And while the discussion went on, Logan stared down the ice at the kid. Bram Ridout had pulled off his mask. His face was red and slick with sweat. The kid looked like he was about to throw up, but upon seeing Logan's gaze Ridout managed a thin sneer and covered his face with the blood-red, three-eyed, lightning-filled mask.

Phone calls were made, with the result that the hockey game would be resumed at five-thirty in the afternoon.

When Logan was told, he cursed mightily.

Logan loved his Saturdays. On Saturdays he owned the Dove Hotel, getting there promptly at noon and not leaving until the law forced him out onto the snowy streets around two in the morning. Logan would play pool, watch TV and neck with ugly women. He would lose at arm-wrestling to cripples and old farts. He would listen to anyone's life story, sing filthy songs and tell filthier jokes. Although this sounds like the ultimate in hacking around, Saturdays at the Dove were the only times Logan felt like he was doing anything worthwhile.

Still, it wasn't likely they would play for very long. Logan had a feeling the kid was going to let in a soft one.

Joe Fineweather seemed to read the thought telepathically. He pointed at Logan gravely. "The child has magic, too," he said, "and Yahoo can't do everything."

"Okay, okay, I give up," said Logan. "What is this *yahoo* stuff?"

"Yahoo," repeated Uncle Joe evenly, giving a nod toward Logan's right shoulder.

Stupidly, Logan turned and looked.

"Yahoo," repeated Joe Fineweather, although upon more intent listening, Logan realized that Uncle Joe was saying something that can't be properly transcribed, hints of *w*s and *r*s floating like twigs in a pond.

"Uncle Joe thought you might need some help last night," explained Jay, "so he gave you a protector."

"A protector?" Logan turned once more to examine the emptiness above his right shoulder.

"You know," shrugged Jay, "like a guardian angel or something." Jay lit a cigarette and pointed at the emptiness with it. "They all got different names. I got one named Papu. I never heard of Yahoo before."

"Yahoo is one of the better ones." Uncle Joe smiled fondly in the spirit's direction. "Very fucking powerful."

"What's he look like?" asked Logan.

"Cute," answered Joe Fineweather.

"What is he, like a bird or what?"

Uncle Joe had to give it some thought. He stared at the space above Logan's shoulder and pursed his lips. "A little like a bird," he decided. "Except for it's got fur. And pointy teeth."

Logan wasn't about to look this time, mostly out of fear that he might actually see such a thing. "Thanks bunches, Uncle Joe," he said uncertainly.

Joe waved this gratitude away humbly. "Let's go inside and have some coffee," he said to the boys. "And then at one o'clock we can watch 'Star Trek.'

∞   ∞   ∞

Kristal woke up when the television set issued forth familiar theme music. She opened her eyes and watched the Starship *Enterprise* roar through the galaxy. Kristal muttered the monologue along with the voice-over. Then she watched about ten seconds of the episode itself and announced, "Seen it."

Kristal had been a science-fiction fan since she was about eleven. It had started on one of the family's many moves; she got bored on the bus and her older brother impatiently tossed her #23 in a series of books about a galactic explorer named Mars Murphy. Little Kristal had fallen instantly in love with the red-bearded spaceman. When things got rough, when it looked like the universe was about to get blasted into nothingness, Mars Murphy would laugh. *His devilish laugh*, the books always said.

The first book, #23 in a series, was called *Attack of the Dogstar People*. Kristal only vaguely remembered the plot—some people from something called the Serious Dogstar attacked. She recalled the dream she'd had the next night. Her father had been traded once more, not to a National Hockey League team but to a team that played up on the Serious Dogstar. The family flew there in a spaceship, piloted by a man in a busdriver's uniform who was rude to them. Everyone on the Dogstar was a dog. That didn't bother Kristal. What bothered her was that everyone on the Serious Dogstar was *serious*. No one laughed or even smiled, and when Kristal tried to do something childish and whimsical they punished her seriously. It was a grim dream, and when Kristal awoke she picked up the book to read about Mars Murphy. Mars Murphy, laughing even when his asteroid cruiser was about to get pulverized by those very same Dogstar people. Ever since then she'd been a sci-fi fan.

In this particular episode of "Star Trek" (which Kristal had seen before) Captain James T. Kirk fell in love with a woman, little suspecting that she was, in fact, the creation of a genius even smarter than little Anthony O'Toole. When Captain Kirk found out that she was, in fact, merely a humanoid, he stopped loving her—and she died of a broken heart.

Kristal said, "Tell me about it," but she wasn't really watching. Kristal was dreaming about laughter. She was also wondering if she and Logan had been attacked by people from the Serious Dogstar.

Seven

Captain James T. Kirk returned to the Starship *Enterprise* a broken man, his heart filled with pain. His friend Mr. Spock, the Vulcan who resists emotion (but can't avoid it; his mother was an Earthling), waited until Captain Kirk fell asleep and then performed a Vulcan mindmeld. Spock drew the pain from his friend Jim into himself. Mr. Spock would have to live with it forever – Captain Kirk could forget.

Jay Fineweather clucked his tongue. "Boy oh boy," he muttered.

"What a guy!" said Uncle Joe.

Logan burst into tears. Savage, burning tears even though it was only two in the afternoon and no one was singing "Try to Remember."

Buck Tanager's face filled the screen. "Let's watch this asshole," Uncle Joe Fineweather said. "That should cheer Logan up."

Uncle Joe was right. As soon as Logan saw Buck Tanager he wiped away tears so that they would no longer blur his vision.

Buck Tanager was sitting in front of a plywood backdrop painted to suggest a split-log cabin. A sign hung underneath a little window: BEAVER LODGE. Buck Tanager was supposedly the owner of a hunting and fishing camp with that name.

Every week Buck Tanager featured a guest in the "adventure." They were usually just friends of his, bankers and businessmen, although some of the Falcons had agreed to it, and sometimes the guest was a *bona fide* celebrity. Two years earlier Buck had somehow convinced Telly Savalas to do the show. Savalas sat in front of the painted backdrop scowling bitterly. He scratched at his bald head and spoke not a word.

That week's guest, Logan was delighted to find out, was the news guy, King McGee. Even though he knew that the outdoor footage had been filmed earlier in the week, Logan was hoping that the two would go hunting and blow each other to bits.

Buck Tanager rocked leisurely in his good old rocking chair, chewing gently on a plug of tobacco. His Stetson fell well over his brow, covering his eyes, Logan reflecting that they didn't make cowboy hats for pinheads.

Beside him, King McGee stared straight into the camera, his face twisted and pimpled. McGee's florid face always seemed to be an aspect of lava flows. King McGee reminded Logan, suddenly, of an ugly little kid in his home town, a kid who tormented his family more than most people (and that was going some). King McGee had tried to look sporty, wearing denim jeans and cowboy boots. His shirt pictured a brocade bucking bronco across the entire front. King McGee had buttoned the shirt all the way up to and including the collar. He had seven ballpoint pens in the pocket.

"It's King McGeek!" enthused Logan. "He's the guy who bites the heads off Scottish mice!" He turned up the sound so that the room was full of the two men talking.

Ol' Buck said, "Well, King-boy, we had ourselves quite a romp out there in the great Ontario outdoors, now din't we?"

And the voice that had once said, "THOU SHALT NOT COMMIT ADULTERY" now said, "WE SURE DID, MR. TANAGER. IT IS JUST A GREAT PLACE TO BE."

Logan imagined them in the great Ontario outdoors. He deprived them of guns and other means of survival and doused them liberally with wolf musk.

"Just before we show the film of our adventure," Buck Tanager was saying, "we should talk about somethin' else. *Hooo*-eeey! Wasn't that a helluva gangbusting fooferaw down to the ol' Coliseum last night?"

Logan flew toward the set to turn the channel, but Jay stuck out a foot and tripped him. "Leave it," Jay suggested.

The camera zoomed in on Buck Tanager's face. "Friends," said Buck, "I guess most folks go to shinny games to see goals get scored. But last night they had just about the most exciting little game of hockey that I ever did see, and the score was egzackly goose-egg to goose-egg. My Falcons and the Hope Blazers fought it out through regalation time and come up tied tight as a knot, no goals a side. Then they played—listen up, neighbours—not one, not two, not three, but *four* periods of overtime and not one single little goal got scored. So who won?" demanded Tanager rhetorically. "We don't know. We's igorant. Because that ol' rulebook say, plain as a cow on a clothesline, no ties allowt. We gone finish that game today. That's right. That there game is going into its fifth period of overtime at five-thirty this P.M."

Joe Fineweather muttered, "Sudden-death overtime. Regulation time. Why don't they just shut up about it?"

Buck Tanager said, "If y'all want to be part of the excitement, get yerself down to the ol' Coliseum. Admission is the same as always, a bargain at six bucks."

"Scumbag," said Logan.

The camera dollied back until it pictured both men sitting in their rocking chairs out in front of Beaver Lodge. Buck said, "Let's hear your thoughts on that game, King-boy."

King McGee took a piece of paper out of his pocket and began to give the views of little Anthony O'Toole. Anthony kept them simple so that people would believe they were

King's views, and King's almighty voice certainly lent the views credibility.

"LAST NIGHT I SAW A STAR BEING BORN. NO ONE KNOWS MUCH ABOUT HIM, BUT I KNOW WHERE HE IS GOING – TO THE NATIONAL HOCKEY LEAGUE. ALL WE KNOW ABOUT HIM IS HIS NAME, BRAM RIDOUT, AND HIS POSITION, GOALTENDER. SIXTY-FIVE SHOTS WERE FIRED AT HIM, AND NOT ONE WAS ALLOWED IN THE NET. VICTOR PHERESFORD FIRED AT HIM POINT-BLANK ON THREE OCCASIONS, AND EVEN THAT MIGHTY MARKSMAN WAS THWARTED. JAY FINEWEATHER, FOR ALL HIS FINESSE AND POISE, COULD NOT PENETRATE RIDOUT'S ARMOUR."

"Hey," said Jay happily, "guess who's got finesse and poise?"

"IT WAS BREATHTAKING, IT WAS MIRACULOUS, IT WAS AWESOME!" King McGee left a dramatic silence. "AT THE OTHER END OF THE RINK, THE STORY WAS THE STELLAR DEFENSIVE WORK OF THE FALCON BACKENDERS!"

"The *what*?!" roared Logan.

"HUFFMAN, MACKIE, QUINN AND OGILVIE ARE QUALITY PLAYERS. THE SHOTS THEY LET BY DIDN'T HAVE ALL THAT MUCH ON THEM. NOW, I CERTAINLY DON'T MEAN TO SAY THAT MR. LOGAN WAS LUCKY – ALTHOUGH HE CERTAINLY *WAS* LUCKY ON MORE THAN ONE OCCASION – BUT WE MUST BEAR IN MIND THAT HE WAS A PROFESSIONAL GOALTENDER AND IS NOT WITHOUT A CERTAIN VESTIGIAL TALENT. BUT WE SHOULD ALSO FACE THE FACT THAT HE HAS BAD KNEES, CERTAIN MENTAL DISORDERS AND A PROBLEM WITH . . ."

King McGee made a fist and popped his thumb out at the top. He used this to gesture almost obscenely toward his mouth.

"HE MAY HAVE PLAYED WELL LAST NIGHT, BUT IN MY OPINION IT IS BRAM RIDOUT WHO WILL EMERGE VICTORIOUS THIS AFTERNOON."

Buck Tanager chewed on that for a while, nodding and saying, "Yep. Yep. Hell, yes. Makes sense, sure as shooting." Then he looked at King McGee and said, "Hey, King ol' feller, can I ask you a question that I been wonderin' about?"

"CERTAINLY."

"I was wonderin'," asked Buck, pointing at King's piece of paper, "why you write your notes in crayon?"

King McGee slipped the paper into his pocket sheepishly. "JUST A HABIT."

Logan sat in his chair smouldering, trying to think of suitable revenge. Part of him was content to sit still, for in truth he had only been accused of being a deranged ex-NHLer with otherworldly knees and a drinking problem. Compared to some aspects of Logan's life, these were plusses.

Suddenly there was a loud explosion, and the television screen fragmented and then sucked itself into itself almost slowly. Logan and Jay Fineweather spun around to see Uncle Joe standing with a twelve-gauge shotgun and a long grin.

Jay scowled. "Eighth set this year," he informed Logan.

∞ ∞ ∞

Anthony O'Toole also watched "The Buck Tanager Adventure Hour," because he had foreknowledge that the game would be discussed, that his views would be expounded through the mouth of Mr. McGee. Ordinarily, Anthony would never have considered watching, because he despised hunting and fishing. Not that he'd ever done either. Fishing intrigued him slightly because of the topological qualities of lakes. It might be nice, he reflected, to sit in a boat and interpolate fundamental coherence based on planar irregularities. He was possessed of this insight:

$$\frac{\Sigma(x3 \neq y) < \Sigma (x3 = y)}{x \div y}$$

That's where you would catch fish.

Anthony listened to his views and was confused. King McGee said some things that Anthony hadn't written. For example, what was this about *mental disorders*? Mr. Logan had no mental disorders as far as Anthony knew. And what had Mr. McGee meant by the odd gesture he'd made, sticking his thumb into the air and poking it into his mouth? Finally, while Anthony had made the prediction re Ridout's victory, it had been predicated on probability theory, statistical interpretation, not on personal disparagement of Mr. Logan.

If there had been anyone in the room, Anthony would have set the record straight. As it was, he was all alone. Pookie, his mother's miniature poodle, lay sleeping some feet away, and Anthony felt an urge to pick the thing up and address his comments to it. As soon as the urge passed, Anthony felt ashamed.

Anthony O'Toole also had information that he had *withheld* from King McGee. Little Anthony had made some phone calls – to a hospital in Atlanta, to the Georgia State Police – and now knew the cause and extent of Logan's knee injuries. Little Anthony wasn't sure why he was keeping it a secret. All he knew was, Logan may be what they termed a *bum*, but given his knees, it was remarkable that the man was playing at all. Anyone sensible would have given up. Although no one ever accused Mr. Logan of being sensible.

Suddenly, Anthony O'Toole giggled. He covered his mouth with both hands. Anthony O'Toole quickly thought of explanations; perhaps there had been a spasm in his windpipe. He was able to convince himself that the giggle had nothing whatsoever to do with his ruminations about the Falconbridge goaltender.

Anthony went to put on his galoshes. His Oxfords occupied them like inhabitants of the serious Dogstar Sirius.

Little Anthony O'Toole would have to walk very slowly to waste the more than two hours before they iced the puck.

∞   ∞   ∞

Jay Fineweather drove Logan into town. Jay hummed under his breath and drummed on the steering wheel. He took sidelong glances at Logan and smiled occasionally. "Hey," Jay said, "you see in the paper this morning how Olver cleared waivers?"

"Lindy cleared waivers?"

"Yeppers. On account of he's a disruptive force in the dressingroom."

Logan grinned despite himself. In the old days Lindy had marched into dressingrooms loaded down with cocaine, ludes and marijuana. No one called him *disruptive* then. But ever since being Born Again, Lindy had been bad news. Now not a single team in the NHL wanted him, despite his obvious talent.

Logan was reminded of Round River, and of Lindy on the ice, in the dawn. He hastened to add the memory of Kristal's laughing breasts, and for one minute and six seconds, Logan was happy.

Then Jay stopped the car and poked him in the arm. "We here, Jack."

Logan turned and saw the Coliseum. Logan sighed wearily.

∞   ∞   ∞

There weren't many people at the Coliseum. The crowd was, at best, a tenth of what it had been the night before. Despite Buck Tanager's last-minute attempts at publicity, most of the fans from the night before assumed that the game had ended in a tie. As well, many who knew about the game stayed away because they shared a like opinion, namely, that within five minutes a goal would be scored. Controversy raged as to which goaltender would emerge victorious. Bram Ridout had a strong legion of supporters, but a surprising number backed Logan. "Hey, I know he's a bum," they'd say. "But it's just that I got this *feeling*."

∞   ∞   ∞

They didn't have Happy Hour on Saturday at Birds of a Feather. Perhaps Mr. Palermo operated on the assumption that everybody was happy on Saturdays anyway. Mr. Palermo possessed a sort of Old World optimism.

That gave Kristal all Saturday afternoon to do her chores. Once she elected to rise from the easy chair (which was midafternoon, the television screen swarming with men involved in sports and games, a spectacle Kristal couldn't watch without thinking of Logan), she threw herself into chore-doing with an alarming vitality. That's what growing up in Holiday Inns will do — Kristal Donahue relished mundane little household duties. She puttered contentedly, watering her plants, dusting, doing laundry and dishes, clipping shopping coupons, copying recipes — though she never cooked, being fed nightly at the club, Kristal had amassed an encyclopaedic volume of culinary delights — and then she decided it was time for a walk.

The skies over Falconbridge were grey, sliced with cloud. A moon, dull and indistinct, God's big messy thumbprint, was stuck in the middle of the welkin. It occurred to Kristal that the moon did not rise and set these days, it merely waited out the day stuck off to the side, ready to move front and centre when the weak sun finally collapsed behind Owsley Mountain. The sun was doing that now, shuddering and sinking. Its light reflected off the ice on Round River and hit the buildings that were Falconbridge. The buildings had mostly to do with commerce — a bank, a grocery, a hardware store. There was the Dove Hotel, its crude rendering of the bird of peace waving in the stiff wind. People pushed by Kristal, their step quickened by the winter's day, headed for the Coliseum. Kristal sighed and returned to her apartment.

∞   ∞   ∞

Big George Tyack grinned. His eyes lit up like stars. George assembled the Falcons in the middle of the dressingroom. He insisted that they be naked; the coach himself was as naked as he'd been at birth. Several of the players coyly tried to wear their jockstraps, but the coach made them take them off.

"Now," said Big George, "everybody join hands and form a great big naked human circle!"

The Falconbridge Falcons didn't want to join hands and form a great big naked human circle. They turned and stared at one another, sullen and bewildered.

"Hey, come on, guys!" bellowed Coach Tyack.

Gingerly, some of the players touched fingers. Big George grabbed Logan's hand on his right and Jay's on his left. Jean-Guy Cabot, outgoing and eager, took his neighbours' hands firmly. "You are going there!" he exclaimed. "And be I not still a manly male creature?"

Finally, the Falconbridge Falcons formed a great big naked human circle. They stood that way for a full five minutes before Big George whispered, "Let's go score us a goal."

Jean-Guy Cabot seemed to draw energy from the great big naked human circle. In Coach Tyack's opinion, Jean-Guy had a lot of potential, not only as a hockey player but as a believer in weird shit. Jean-Guy took to the ice with a kind of black fire playing in his eyes. In the first minute he grabbed the puck, took it into the Hope zone, swung around a rather flat-footed defenceman and proceeded unmolested toward the net. Jean-Guy cranked up well in advance. The crowd fell silent. Jean-Guy's slapshot had a reputation for skull-shattering velocity. Jean-Guy smacked it, the puck sailed invisibly for the top right-hand side of the net.

Bram Ridout's stick hand lashed out furiously, the action of someone who is bothered by a mosquito. The puck bounced off his blocker and onto the ice. Unfortunately for the kid, it fell right onto the stick of Jean-Guy, who never stopped for much once he got started. Jean-Guy craftily tapped the puck along the ice toward the open side of the net.

With a melodramatic abandonment of life and limb, the kid collapsed to the ice. Magically, he fell on top of the puck, just as that little piece of rubber was about to cross the goal-line.

After the whistle went, ending the play, Logan found himself beating his stick on the ice in time with the applause from the stands.

Logan decided that when the game was through, he would go to Birds of a Feather and visit with Kristal and Koko. It could be a blessing in disguise, this unexpected play on a Saturday, because Logan could show up at the bar early and sober. He made a mental note to hurry home and shave, so that he could enter the establishment early, sober and well groomed. Logan further determined to nurse beer all night long, consuming at most four, and to sit smiling and dry-eyed through a rendition of "Try to Remember." He hoped he would be able to tell Kristal that he won the game for the Falcons. Logan decided that if he managed to get Kristal to bed, he would merely hold her tightly all night long.

Logan was pleased with his resolve.

He caught a puck and returned it to the ice nonchalantly.

Eight

Logan entered Birds of a Feather sometime around eleven o'clock that evening.

He was not cleanshaven.

Logan's legs were completely under the power of his otherworldly knees. If Logan wanted to stand one place, his legs decided they wanted to go somewhere else. Should Logan be walking, his legs would decide to stop dead and Logan would have to reach out quickly, supporting himself on the backs of chairs and people's heads.

Logan somehow convinced his legs to take him to the stand-up bar and the deed was done relatively smartly. Logan grinned at the barmaid. She regarded him archly. "Yes, Logan?"

Logan laughed the laugh of a man with great resolve. "Beer," he answered. "But only four, tops."

"You want four beers?"

"Yep." Logan reached for his wallet. "Then I won't bother you no more. I'm going to nurse these here beers. No serious alcohol or nothing." Logan threw about half his weekly salary in the woman's direction. "There you go. Keep the change."

The barmaid bent over to retrieve the bills from the floor. Logan pulled himself across the bar so that he could peek down the front of her cocktail waitress outfit. When the barmaid

70

stood up, Logan remarked, astutely, "I think I should have shaved."

The barmaid was counting the money. "Logan," she said quietly, "you gave me over fifty dollars."

"Not enough?" Logan reached for his wallet.

"Dork," said the barmaid, sticking the greater part of the wad back into Logan's pocket.

"When does Kristal start her set?" asked Logan suddenly.

"In a few minutes," was the answer.

Logan swung his head around, seeing who else was at the bar. There was a woman standing not three feet from him. Logan's hard-on declared a state of emergency. His brain slapped itself into readiness and his heart ran for cover. It was Darla Featherstone, the perfect weather/social calendar woman.

Logan had seen Darla in person only once before. She'd attended a Falcons home game, in the company of Elmore Daisy pretending to be Buck Tanager. This started vicious rumours circulating amongst the team, but Logan gave them no credence.

Darla was sipping a Birdbath, the house special of Birds of a Feather, a concoction of sweet liquors served in a vessel that, while smallish for a birdbath, was enormous for a drink. She was smoking a long cigarette, the filter end a violent blood-red because of her lipstick.

Logan edged along the bar until he was standing right beside her. "Excuse me," Logan said politely.

Darla Featherstone levelled a look at Logan that almost made his hard-on scamper away in terror. Her eyes were as black as pitch.

"Um . . .," began Logan.

Darla Featherstone opened her mouth and there came a scream that plunged the bar into a frightened silence. It was a rough-edged howl, thick and inhuman, and it bit deep into the bone. There wasn't a square inch of flesh in that room that

71

wasn't covered with goosepimples except for that which wrapped Logan.

Logan forgot about Darla immediately. He screamed back, making almost the same sound; Logan was unable, however, to keep a suggestion of humanity out of it. Then Logan began to move his neck quickly back and forth. His legs, caught up in the spirit of the thing, commenced to walk him around in small, tribal circles.

The military cockatoo clung to the side of his cage, his talons gripping the bars hard, and imitated Logan's head movements. The bird screamed again, more defiantly, knowing that it had an audience. Logan mimicked the howl, inspiring Koko to new heights. The bird jumped backwards, onto its perch, as if it needed more room for added lung power. Koko ruffled his plumage a bit, sending ripples up and down his length, and then went for the big one. Koko turned instantly redder as the sound came out of his beak. This howl was so wonderful that at least half the people in the bar plugged their ears.

Logan was no quitter. He saw the wisdom in free space, so he climbed energetically onto the bar. If Logan had had any plumage he would have rumpled it splendidly, but as it was he merely shrugged his overcoat off his shoulders and loosened his woollen scarf. Logan poked his head to and fro in a birdlike manner, the better to clear his windpipe of any obstruction. His howl (the uncontested winner) was twenty seconds old and still going strong when Kristal came into the room and sat down at the piano.

Logan ended the scream abruptly and grinned from his perch. He feared that things were not going according to plan. He deeply regretted his attendance at the Dove Hotel earlier that evening. Logan wished instead that he'd gone home and shaved.

Kristal stroked out some soft misshapen chords that roiled like snakes.

"Hi, Kristal!" chirped Logan. There was no way of getting down from the bar without leaping from it or crawling down on hands and knees. Neither seemed like a good idea.

Kristal played a few more chords, rapid ones that went through some bizarrely twisted changes. The music made Logan uneasy. "Hi," Kristal said. She struck something hard and dissonant. "Who won the game?"

Everyone in the place turned to look at Logan.

Logan began to feel quite dizzy, so he gingerly lowered himself to his knees and groped along the bar until he bumped into Darla's Birdbath. He poured about half of it into his mouth and then lay down. "Nobody," he mumbled quietly.

Nasty chords rang out from the piano. "Nobody?"

Logan swung his legs over the side of the bar and after two or three attempts managed to sit upright. "Know what, know what?" Logan demanded loudly. "It's the longest hockey game ever. We already played . . ." Logan waggled fingers in front of his bleary eyes, hoping to inspire his brain to mathematical exercise. "Six . . . no, *seven* periods of overtime. And the old record was only six. So we are the longest hockey players. Call the Guinness Book!" Logan fell off the bar. "What a fucking kid. Lucky for me I got Yahoo." Logan pulled himself upright by means of a support pole. "Yahoo!" he sang out musically, adding, "When I have a couple little drinky-poos the manky little fucker flies away. At least, I figure he flies, 'cause he looks like a bird. Except for the fur and teeth. It's complicated." Logan remembered that the only reason he was in Birds of a Feather was that he loved Kristal, so he said, "Why are we talking? We should be listening to my sweetheart. Kristal, sing us a song." Logan stuck out an elbow and toppled backwards. Miraculously the elbow caught the lip of the bar and held him up.

Kristal swept out a few quick changes, alien and menacing. Logan thought he detected something familiar in them. Kristal opened her mouth and the hole in Logan's heart began to ache, a phantom pain.

Kristal sang, "*Try to remember when life was so tender . . .*"

Logan tried desperately to escape.

73

"That no one wept except the willow . . ."

Logan flew toward the exit and collided with a pillar. He bounced back and landed on the table of a middle-aged couple who were smiling and holding hands.

"Try to remember when life was so tender that dreams were kept beside your pillow . . ."

The sight of the couple holding hands fragmented him totally.

"Try to remember when life was so tender that love was an ember about to billow . . ."

Logan sprawled across the table and blubbered.

Kristal sang in a lonely way.

"Try to remember and if you remember—"

The middle-aged couple were drinking Birdbaths. Logan had knocked one of them over when he landed, but he grabbed the survivor and sucked at it greedily.

"—then follow."

Soon the song was finished. It received good-natured applause from the patrons, all of whom had ignored Logan's histrionics. Logan brushed away his tears and stood, weaving but upright. "Well, I think I'll just be moseying along," he announced, mostly for the benefit of his legs, who were still under the influence of the knees. "Yeppers," Logan repeated, "I think I'll head out." His legs got the hint and after a bit of negotiation with the knees began a wobbly approach of the exit. "Bye-bye!" called Logan, thrilled to find himself in motion.

"Logan!" called out Kristal.

Logan walked out the door. He had desperately wanted to stop at the sound of her voice, but his legs were on a roll. So it was with an aching heart (one with a hockey-puck-sized hole in it) that Logan allowed himself to be carried out the door to the Dove Hotel.

∞   ∞   ∞

Leaving Kristal Donahue miserable and not a little angry. She decided she would indeed pen the song, "He's a goof," regardless of how strapped she got for rhymes. Besides, couplets were popping into her mind at a dizzying clip: "He's a goof, I wish he'd go *poof!*" "He's a goof, and I've got the proof." Kristal banged out something that sounded like free-form jazz only weird, violating the piano for more than a minute, ruthless and evil. She stopped when a laugh filled the barroom.

Kristal looked up.

Her first thought was that Mars Murphy had parked his intergalactic spacepod outside Birds of a Feather and come in for a brew. The man (occupying the entrance and laughing) was immense, muscular and sported a long red beard. This man wore an enormous buffalo-skin coat. He'd pulled it open so that his sweater was visible. There, written in letters that appeared to be fashioned from flame, was the word HOPE.

Kristal realized, a tad testily, that the Hope-man was laughing at the way she was playing piano. She dished a black look in his direction and got her hands to play "Feelings." Kristal hated "Feelings" more than any other song, but her hands seemed to like it.

The huge bearded man sat at the piano bar. He crossed his arms and leaned over, cradling his head and gazing at Kristal. Kristal gave him a quick, tiny smile, the same smile she gave to everyone who sat at the piano bar.

Vicky the waitress approached, asked the bearded man what he wanted. The man answered by presenting Vicky with an imaginary object about the size of a beer bottle.

"What kind?" asked Vicky.

The bearded man made a loud farting sound and shrugged. He gesticulated with the invisible beer bottle.

"How about a Carlsberg?" asked Vicky.

"Chest." The man nodded and propelled Vicky toward the bar.

Kristal finished playing "Feelings" and segued into "Rain-drops Keep Falling on My Head," another of her hands' favourites. Kristal had fairly good taste in music, but the same can't be said of her hands.

When the Hope-man realized that "Feelings" was over he applauded energetically. "Chest!" he bellowed, stomping his feet. "Chest!"

Kristal stole a quick peek downward, making sure nothing had fallen out. The bearded man paused for a moment, tilting his head toward the piano. He seemed to recognize "Raindrops Keep Falling on My Head" because he smiled very broadly and pointed to his own head, miming with the other how raindrops kept falling on it.

The man did a pantomime for every song Kristal played, although he did use the occasional prop. When she played "Yesterday," for example, the Hope-man pulled out a little pocket calendar and flipped through it backwards. When Kristal played "I Left My Heart in San Francisco" he pretended to disembowel himself. And through it all he bellowed "Chest!" At the end of her set Kristal conducted a little experiment. She did a reprise of "Try to Remember (the Kind of September)."

The bearded Hope-man grinned and winked at Kristal. He reached up, scratched his head (trying to remember) and then shrugged his massive shoulders to indicate that he hadn't been able to.

Then he laughed.

Even if you aren't Mars Murphy, thought Kristal, *you'll do.*

DAY THREE

Nine

" Is no Earthling brave enough to defend his world against Zortron?"

In Logan's dreams, Zortron was an insect-like creature, multi-limbed and oily black. His head was covered with an enchanted shield, a mask; lightning forked from all sides, and there were holes for three smouldering eyes.

The metallic voice continued its taunting. "Is no Earthling brave enough to defend his world against Zortron?"

Logan opened his eyes. High above were rows of fluorescent lights. Logan turned his head and fell off the plastic chairs he had been sleeping on. His knees smashed into the tiled floor and counterattacked by racking his poor body with pain.

"Is no Earthling brave enough to defend his world against Zortron?"

Logan, on hands and alien knees, snarled, "Fucking right, Zortron. I'll tear you from limb to limb, you manky extraterrestrial."

Logan pulled himself into a chair and took a look at his surroundings. He recognized it as a bus terminal. Unfortunately, bus terminals tend to much of a muchness.

"First things first," said Logan. His head ached, but it was insulated by a layer of booze that had yet to wear off. Which is to say, Logan was still half cut. He reached into his pockets and drew out a handful of change.

"Is no Earthling—"

Logan plucked a quarter off his palm and bellowed. "Zortron dies! I shall make the earth safe for the lovely Kristal and her offspring!"

Logan pursued the sound of the voice into a hallway.

There he saw it—a large black box adorned with galaxies.

Logan gazed at the large coloured screen. An alien's face, formidable and hideous, stared back at him. This creature once more issued its challenge: "Is no Earthling brave enough to defend himself against Zortron?"

"Sorry, Zorry. You've met your match. It is Logan of the Planet Earth, third stone from the Sun, aided and abetted by his otherworldly knees, themselves perilous mindfuckers from the Dogstar Sirius!" Logan rammed a quarter into the belly of the machine. It gurgled happily and the alien's face disappeared. The screen filled with the place of battle, the huge starfield that contains both the homeworld of Zortron and our own little blue rock. "Here we shall fight," the unseen Zortron informed Logan, "with lasers and time-reversal units."

"I'm an old hand at this," Logan informed the contraption. "Just try sending one of your kamikaze lunarsailers this way."

Something that looked like a Viking vessel with grotesquely oversized sails came floating onto the screen. With a low electronic rumble it let loose a torpedo-like projectile. Logan activated his time-reversal unit and timed a laser assault perfectly, exploding the lunar needle just as it was about to leave (*enter* in reversed time) the lunarsailer. The vessel exploded into dots of light.

"Not bad," commented Zortron. "But have you guile enough for my black hole skipper?" A curiously innocent capsule floated into view. Logan knew it was very dangerous—the time-reversal unit was ineffective against it, because the skipper circumvented time by travelling through a network of black holes. Logan waited until the skipper disappeared from sight and then fired his laser at the point where the black hole must have been. Logan then waited until there was the faintest glimmer on the screen (which had to be the skipper re-entering) and activated the time-reversal. With a perfect shot Logan closed this other exit, thereby consigning the skipper to travel forever in the netherworld between the two black holes.

"Ouch!" said Zortron angrily.

Logan laughed, and felt good that he was winning.

If it came down to it, Logan would die defending his world.

∞   ∞   ∞

Kristal Donahue was not aware of the term *synchronicity* (Kristal had encountered the word but dodged it, instinctively wary of language that seemed to be up to something), so she didn't recognize the following examples of it:

a) The bearded Hope-man's name, while not Mars, was *Lars*.
b) His last name was *Løkan*.
c) Like Logan, Løkan was a hockey player, although he played for the Hope Blazers.
d) Løkan was twenty-three years old. He'd scored twenty-three points that season. His uniform number was twenty-three. Twenty-three was the number of words in Lars Løkan's English vocabulary (with a certain amount of latitude, accepting *chest* for *yes*, etc.). And, unless Kristal missed her guess, twenty-three was the number of times Lars Løkan intended making love to her before lunch.

At the moment, Lars was asleep. His mouth hung open stupidly and huge simooms blasted in and out. Kristal snuck out of bed, wrapping a blanket around her and tiptoeing into her kitchen. Kristal noticed, on top of her refrigerator, the long silver bird-whistle. She opened the kitchen window.

Kristal remarked inwardly that she was experiencing nothing resembling guilt, although life and its various complications made her feel queasy. Skittish. Any sudden noise and Kristal was sure she'd bolt for the door. This was Logan's doing. Kristal had long had a reputation as a docile, placid woman; Logan had reduced her to a coltish creature with a perpetual tremor in her long legs.

Kristal tooted the long silver bird-whistle into the frozen town of Falconbridge.

∞   ∞   ∞

In the end—which came a full two hours later—Zortron abandoned his plan to destroy the earth. "You are the most valiant protector your blue stone has had this week," the machine informed Logan, "and I shall allow you to inscribe your name on the list of Great Heroes." A series of instructions lit up on the screen, instructing Logan how to spell out his name. The list of Great Heroes appeared. The blank spot left for Logan was number one, and his score beside it was a full hundred thousand more than number two's, who's name was JOEY. Logan carefully and slowly spelled out LOGAN and then set about finding out where he was.

At least the world was safe.

Logan prowled clumsily about the bus terminal searching for clues. He realized that there should have been a ticket-seller and -taker behind the counter, but Logan and Zortron seemed to be alone in the place.

Logan was startled to hear a thick gasping followed by a hoary release of breath. This combination was repeated some moments later. Logan searched out the sound, and found the source sitting more or less upright in an orange plastic chair. The source was a small man, grey-haired, possessed of a derelict furze. His coat was ancient and threadbare, and couldn't possibly have battled the bitter air. His shoes seemed to be held together by slush. The man snored again and Logan caught in the release the decayed odour of used alcohol.

The man's face, even in slumber, was the saddest Logan had ever seen. The man's face had given itself over to misery without a struggle, the lines deep with worry.

And every breath now sounded to Logan like a sigh.

The man's fingers, gnarled and twisted, sat diligently on top of a box on his lap. While the rest of his body slept, the man's fingers entwined with the rope, keeping the box shut.

Logan sat down on an orange plastic chair and prodded the man; the man snored through. Logan tried an elbow-prod next; that caused a snore-in-progress to falter for a moment. Finally Logan grabbed the little man by the shoulders and shook him violently. Logan had some notion that when the man woke up he would look around with a wide grin and sparkling eyes.

When the man woke up he was just as sad but more animated about it. His eyes were the most beaten thing about him, dull and exanimate. The sad man looked at the closest wall, he looked at Logan, he let his lids fall shut. Logan poked the sad man until he got a half-woken "Huh?"

"Where are we?"

After a moment the man opened one of his dead eyes and allowed it to skip around the environs quickly. He tucked it back into his face and responded, "Souse Grouth." A second later he was snoring.

South Grouse.

It made Logan ill to speculate on the twistings of his heart and mind that would lead him to South Grouse in the middle of the night.

Something drew Logan outside the bus terminal. Not very far, just a few steps so that he was gazing toward the north.

There it was. Like a leftover from a grade-B horror flick, the Social Services Rehabilitative Centre—the lunatic asylum —loomed in silhouette against the dawn.

∞   ∞   ∞

Lars Løkan didn't make it to twenty-three times, but he came closer than most chaps would, too close for Kristal's comfort.

Lars and Kristal had breakfast together, sitting naked at the little table, drinking coffee, scraping butter onto toast, browsing through a paper from the day before. Lars Løkan seemed to understand much of what he read. Periodically he would stab at the periodical with a huge forefinger. "Baaggh!!" Lars concentrated on the Sports section. At one point he lifted up a photograph of a Minnesota North Star and pointed to the grainy image of the jersey's crest. Then he pounded his own chest. Kristal was made to understand that he belonged in some way to the Minnesota franchise.

"Cam Hop," explained Lars, "tits rup."

Eventually this was translated by Kristal to mean that he had come to Hope to be taught the ropes.

"Kizzle lak hooker?"

Kristal had a bit of a problem with this one, until she realized that she was being asked if she liked hockey. "Lak hooker mach," she nodded. "Friend play hooker." Kristal had no idea why she mentioned that.

"Frem?" Lars was instantly interested. "Wha frem?"

"Logan," confessed Kristal. She stood up from the table and dropped into a goaltender's crouch.

Lars Løkan's delight knew no bounds. "LOOGAN!" he screamed, clapping his hands together. Lars started speaking in his native tongue, very rapidly, clearly praise for Loogan. "Loogan frem Kizzle," he mused. Lars cocked his eyebrows and regarded Kristal. "Kizzle laf Loogan?"

Kizzle shrugged.

Lars Løkan accepted the shrug without question, even though Kizzle had no idea what it meant. Lars fell upon his breakfast heartily, tossing toast into his mouth. "Loogan," Lars chuckled. Lars Løkan tilted his head back and howled. Kristal intuited that he was doing an imitation of her addled erstwhile lover.

After breakfast Lars told Kristal that he was going to go practice. That took about four minutes. It took Lars half an hour to illicit from Kristal a promise to attend the hockey game — the continuation — that evening. They were going to try to finish it one more time. Kenny Pringle was determined — near obsessed — that the game should have an outright winner, as dictated by his little mimeographed rulebook. Elmore Daisy was determined — definitely obsesssed — to soak people as many times as possible. The Coliseum management — Buck Tanager served as an advisor — had willingly dropped its Sunday night Free Skating and cancelled a couple of Peewee games. Everyone was getting caught up in the Ridout — Logan duel. Everyone except Kristal that is, but, eventually and reluctantly, Kizzle agreed to attend.

Lars made her a promise. "I bit Loogan!" Lars Løkan pretended to unleash a mighty slapshot and he lifted his imaginary stick in triumph as the puck eluded the invisible Loogan.

Kristal nodded. "Uh-yeah" was all she could say.

Ten

Logan crouched and ran across the lawn. When he came near the wall he dove into the shrubbery. Logan felt along the brick until his fingers met a stick that was wedged into the masonry. He grabbed the stone adjacent and started to pull. In a few minutes Logan had created a hole in the thick wall.

Logan crawled through on his belly. He knew that it was too early in the morning – it had just gone seven, the dawn a faint squeak, the inmates were drowsily being led to washrooms and showering pits, white-uniformed drovers bringing up the rear – for anybody to be up to much, so Logan stood upright and took a long look around.

Nothing had changed. That was the power of such places, the changelessness. That was what made people feel comfortable even as the humanity was being yanked out through their noses.

Logan darted across the snow-encrusted lawn to what he knew was the groundskeeper's shed. A plank willingly bent sideways (as Logan knew it would) and soon he re-emerged through the same gap, disguised as one of the groundskeeper's helpers. Logan was wearing overalls, a huge green coat, work gloves, work boots and a work hat. He pulled down the fuzzy flaps of the hat to complete the spectacle. He carried a huge galvanized snowshovel and swaggered in a very plebeian manner. Several orderlies noticed him, but no one paid much attention.

Logan decided to limit his visit to one of the tiny cottages consigned to long-termers and people with very drastic problems. Of these there were twenty-three. Logan counted off thirteen, ditched his snowshovel and ran through a front door.

Logan knew that it would be dark, but he was not prepared for the pitch-blackness that confronted him. His left leg immediately ran into something and his knee tossed him to the ground. On his way down, Logan's jaw made substantial contact with something hard and angular. He heard a scream, a sound like a mouse might make if the mouse was about five feet tall. Logan propped himself up on one elbow and said, "It's all right. Don't get excited. It's only me."

The five-foot-tall mouse whimpered.

"Just little ol' me," repeated Logan soothingly. He carefully lumbered to his feet. "Just the kid. Just me."

A candle was lit. It in turn lit the face of an old man, small and moonlike. The old eyes studied Logan for a time; the old eyes crinkled, the mouth began to smile.

"Back so soon?"

Logan's leg throbbed and didn't want to straighten. Logan whacked at it and answered the old man distractedly. "I'm just, you know, visiting."

The old man raised a trembling hand and gesticulated at Logan's outfit. "And you've got a new job. I'm *so* proud of you."

Logan was wary of doing himself more damage in the darkened room. "Do you think," he asked, "that we could get a little light happening in here?"

"Let there be light," cackled the old man, and there was. The old man had merely flicked a switch on the wall; still, the effect was pretty dramatic.

The room was exactly what Logan had expected, but that

didn't stop him from being surprised. It was a surprising room. It looked, more or less, like his father's library/den had looked when Logan was a little boy. (The room where little Logan had found the ASTRONOMY book that claimed that there were bulls and hunters and diverse things growing out of celestial seeds.) However, this room appeared to have been ravaged by a demented wind. The books were cockeyed and akilter, loose-leaf pages strewn about. Medical charts were tacked to the wall, overlapping, sideways, upside down, charts that detailed the bloodlines and sinewy of everything from the Hairy Blue Eagle to the Great Tusked Guinea Boar. There were globes in the room, an antique globe that was the earth, globes for every planet in our solar system. These were arranged in order, although to the eye they seemed no less chaotic than anything else in the little cottage. In the centre of the room, where the Sun should have been, was a huge writing desk, tilted gently to balance a pot of ink and a quill.

The old man climbed onto a high stool behind this stand. He was dressed in black robes, twice as long again as his tiny frame. On his head there perched a pointed cap, adorned with images of suns and moons and stars. The old man smiled down at Logan and said, "Hello, my son."

Logan nodded. "Hello, Father."

"I'm extremely busy today," said the old man. "*Hellzapoppin'!*"

Logan said, "I can't stay long. I just came to see how you all were doing."

"Let me ask you something," said the old man. "Do you, as a puny human being, a complete sub-normaloid, a meaningless speck on the ocean of creation, do you feel that I'm doing a good job?"

Logan shuffled his feet. "What does it matter what I think?"

The old man stuck a bended finger into the air. "Good point! It doesn't matter one little bit. You are a mere mortal, even less, and I am that I am. But it can't hurt to get the occasional outside opinion."

Logan shrugged, "Everything's going about the same as usual, Pop."

The old man turned nasty. "Do not refer to me as Pop. It's insolent. You call me Father, as in Our Father Who Art. Got that, bubby-boy?"

"Right."

"The same as usual, huh?" The old man rubbed his grizzled chin. "That ain't good. I said it before and I'll say it again, *hellzapoppin'!*"

Logan spun one of the globes absent-mindedly.

The old man screamed and rushed to still the globe. "What are you trying to do? Send everyone careering into the voids of outer space or what?"

"Sorry," muttered Logan.

"Tell me this." The skirt of the old man's robes suddenly blew upwards and he was in motion. "Give me your opinion on that thing I invented, love."

"Pop—" began Logan, but the old man shook a gnarled fist, so Logan began again. "Father, I just came to see how you were, and how Mum was, and how Neppy and Pluto—"

"Why didn't you say so? You've come to the right place. After all, I'm omniscient." The old man had an antique television set in the corner of the room. He dashed over and pulled its on/off switch. The screen filled with a snowy blankness. "Here we go. Now, what was the last name?"

Logan said. "Logan."

"Loganloganlogan..." He spun the channel selector. Nothing changed upon the white screen. "There we go. First name?"

"Edna."

"Ednaednaedna..." The old man fooled with the fine tuning. "Here we are. Edna Logan. She's an old woman, right?"

Logan nodded.

"But, hey!" said Logan's father. "You should have seen her when she was younger. Va-va-voochie! And *built*—my goodness gracious. She seems to be fine. She plays a lot of cards. I think I'll give her some good luck." The old man waved his liver-spotted hand over the screen. "*Bam-zoom!* Gimme another name."

"Neppy."

"Neppy," said the old man in his omniscient way. "That would be shorty for Neptunia, would it not?"

Logan nodded.

"Lovely name. You don't hear that name very often," reflected the old man as he spun the fine tuner. "There she is! Boy, is she big! What a big girl that Neppy is. Let me see here. How is she? She's fine. She's just a little lonely is all. Hey . . ." There was an impish look in the old man's eye. "How about I give her a boyfriend, eh? Any opinion, oh puny one?"

"Good idea."

"*Ippity-bippity-pow!*" chirped the old man, popping his fingers. "Next?"

"Pluto."

"Pluto Logan." The fine tuner was spun. "Here he is! What a good-looking young man. Very handsome. He appears to be . . . singing. Yep, singing. Definitely singing. That's about all he does, apparently."

"He likes to sing," acknowledged Logan.

"You know what the kid needs? He needs a hobby. Like, for example, fishing." The old man made several magical passes over the screen. "*Zip-zip-zappy!!*"

"Thanks very much," muttered Logan.

"Hold on, hold on, there's one left. One named—" The old man said Logan's first name. God only knows Logan's first name.

The old man fooled around with the fine tuning. "He's far away from the rest of them. Why is that?" The old man looked up and his eyes were piercing.

"I don't know," mumbled Logan.

"He plays a game. Hockey. He plays in goal."

"Forget it."

"There is a girl in his life, I see. But . . . oh-oh . . . she's in a bed with someone else. Son-of-a-gun."

"Come on, Pop."

"It's his own damn fault! He's a dumb, stupid pissant! He drinks too much and fucks around!"

"I'm leaving now. I just wanted to know how you were."

"And he's always looking up in the sky! What a maroon! Walking around with his nose stuck up in the sky. Ha-ha-ha!" The old man's laugh was cruel, derisive.

"Yeah, well, that's *your* fault!" shouted Logan. "I'm looking for those fucking constellations, but they aren't there! They're just not there!"

The old man took umbrage. "They most certainly are there. I put them there myself. I put, lemme see, a hunter, and a dog, and I think maybe a unicorn—"

"Nothing! Nothing!"

The old man returned his attention to the blank television screen. "I'll tell you one more thing. Bermondsey is about to come walking through that front door."

The door to the cottage opened. A tall man with a gleaming bald head stood there. He wore black horn-rimmed glasses that distorted his eyes, making them look huge and owl-like. This man crossed his arms and spoke gently. "Hello, Logan."

Logan took a sudden leap, knocking the man, sending him backwards into the snow piled outside the door. Logan jumped over him and continued running.

Logan ran as fast as he could. He went over the wall this time, instead of under it, and soon he was back at the bus station.

∞   ∞   ∞

Logan was a dollar shy of the bus fare back to Falconbridge, but the ticket guy sold him a seat anyway. His explanation, offered in a friendly way, was, "You look like you've had a rough time." Logan realized that he looked like something pointed at

91

by children, shunned by mothers in their linens. ("What's the matter with that man, Mommy? Why does he look like that?" "Never mind, dear.") This pleased Logan immensely. To further the impression he removed his false teeth, peppering both uppers and lowers with gaps. He sat down on an orange plastic chair and grinned at passers-by with an upturned palm. They hurried by with looks of great disgust.

It occurred to Logan that there were lots of passers-by, which was surprising. South Grouse wasn't a great hub of activity at the best of times, let alone on a grey Sunday dawning. Many of the passers-by seemed to know one another, talking here and there in little clutches of three and four. They were mostly men, dressed in trenchcoats and rumpled fedoras. These men smoked cigarettes; indeed, Logan suspected that they were making their way to some cigarette festival.

The bus from Toronto pulled into the bay. Everyone in the terminal moved to board it. Logan joined the crowd. He let spittle drool from the side of his mouth and bent over as though saddled with a misshapen hump. Logan was on the bus in no time, and he ran to the back and claimed a seat next to the toilet. His neighbour, Logan noticed, was a very square little woman.

The bus was already crowded, and became doubly so with the addition of everyone from the South Grouse station. The square woman beside Logan knew almost everybody. She spoke with a husky, asexual voice. "Hi, Bob!" or, "Hey, Dan-Dan!" Her name, Logan discovered, was Mickey.

Mickey was a woman after Logan's own riddled heart. Before the bus pulled away she reached into her trenchcoat pocket and took out a silver flask. Mickey dug an elbow into Logan's side.

"Hey, bud," she spoke in her rough midrange, "care for a little Remy Martin?" Mickey anglicized the name so that it sounded like she was talking about the guy who lives upstairs.

"Oh–" Logan did some calculations. There were many

hours before game time. "Yeah." He took a sip and let the liquor slide into his belly.

"Going to Falconbridge?" asked Mickey, taking a sip herself.

Logan nodded, received back the silver flask.

"Ever been there before?" asked Mickey.

Logan nodded again. "I live there," he offered.

"What's it like?" Mickey's questions tended to be short and pointed.

"It's okay. It's got a nice bar."

This was apparently just the answer Mickey wanted, because she nodded vigorously. She stubbed out her cigarette on the back of the seat in front and immediately whipped out her packet for another. Mickey inhaled and then issued forth a huge billow, much more smoke than she seemed to have drawn in.

"So, are you going to Falconbridge?" Logan asked Mickey, spraying her quite severely on the *f*. Sheepishly, Logan turned his back momentarily and rammed his false teeth back into his mouth. Logan turned and smiled.

"Hey!" noted Mickey. "You're not a bad-looking guy when you got teeth."

Logan accepted the compliment graciously.

"Yeah," said Mickey. "I'm going to Falconbridge. We're all going to Falconbridge. We're going to see what gives with the hockey game. Longest son-of-a-bitch ever."

Logan spat out his teeth and replaced them in his pocket. "Me," he informed Mickey, "I'm a bum."

Logan noticed the sad little man from the bus terminal coming back to use the washroom. He seemed hesitant to put the hatbox down even to open the bathroom door. So Logan pulled the entry open for him; the man smiled sadly.

"The story is the goaltenders," editorialized Mickey. "There's one named Bram Ridout—"

"A fucking kid," Logan footnoted bitterly.

"And the other's name is Logan. Used to play in the NHL. Ever hear of him?"

"I don't think so."

"I looked up his stats," said Mickey. "He's a wanker."

"A wanker, huh?" Logan grabbed the brandy flask out of Mickey's hand and drained about an inch's worth down his gullet.

Mickey retrieved it and polished it off, obviously fearful that it might be her last chance.

"I'll tell you one thing about Logan," said Logan. "He saved the frigging world!"

"Hah?"

"Delirium tremens," Logan explained.

"Yeah, right."

Logan gazed out the window. Along the road were farm people, Sunday-suited and walking quietly to church. This stung Logan. He wished for a simplicity of heart. A tear escaped from within him and rolled down his cheek.

Mickey put her arm around Logan and pulled his head so that it rested on her bosom. "You go to sleep, you bum," she suggested tenderly.

Logan was soon snoring.

∞   ∞   ∞

Logan dreamed uneasily of Darla Featherstone, the perfect weather/social calendar woman. In his dream she was on television, predicting a horrible storm, a fulguration of biblical dimension. Darla was naked. Logan couldn't hear exactly what she was saying, but he knew she was predicting winds that would lash and slap our little blue stone. Darla consulted a map. She turned to point at it and the slumbering Logan marvelled at her bottom. She showed where the storm originated, poked it in the eye, a land Logan had not heard of, its name unpronounceable. Darla turned and smiled; Logan woke up in Falconbridge.

Eleven

Anthony O'Toole wasn't allowed to go out on schoolnights. He wasn't sure whether this dictate was handed down by his mother or his father, and he suspected that neither of them knew either. The rule simply existed. There was no compelling reason for it; unlike other small Falconbridgers, Anthony never trundled down the lane to wait for a yellow schoolbus. Anthony had already graduated high school, had been awarded his bachelor's degree in mathematics, was simply biding time until his fourteenth birthday, at which time he was scheduled to begin postgraduate work at Johns Hopkins. Still, the rule had never proven bothersome, because he had never before had a desire to go out on schoolnights. Anthony's only consistent outing was to Falcon home games on alternate Fridays. However, on this particular Sunday evening, Anthony wanted to go to the Coliseum.

He presented the case quite cogently to his mother. Anthony wished that his father was present, because his father liked hockey and might have been sympathetic. Thinking about it, Anthony couldn't remember seeing Mr. O'Toole for some days.

Mrs. O'Toole sat on the sofa, her legs curled beneath her, and stared at her little son. Her expression was, as always, a step away from aghast. Mrs. O'Toole was terrified of Anthony's massive intellect.

"The occasion is fraught with remarkability, Mater," said Anthony. "Regardless of the outcome, this shall henceforth be noted, asterisked and honoured as the longest professional hockey match ever contested. As you may well know, this distinction previously belonged to a game between the Detroit Red Wings and the Montreal Maroons, 1936, terminated sixteen and one-half minutes into the sixth overtime period."

Something in Mrs. O'Toole's look suggested that she hadn't, in fact, known this.

Anthony cleared his throat and continued. "To be not present at the decision little befits a hockey scholar of my stature. In addition, Mr. McGee has specifically requested my attendance, that I may supply him commentary for the nightly newscast. I will also state for the record that I am exceedingly well rested, having slumbered an additional two hours against this very eventuality. Therefore, Mater, I hereby request that the rule prohibiting my egress on quote-unquote school-nights—it is a matter of some import that I do not, in point of fact, attend school as such, although I labour diligently on my theories of planar instability—be waived on this one extraordinary occasion." Anthony then struck a pose and smiled in a manner that he hoped could be described as angelic.

Mrs. O'Toole said no.

Anthony felt a constriction in his throat muscles. "Ah. I see." Then he felt a quickening of his pulse, a sensation not at all unpleasant. "Yes. Very well. I bow to your judgement, based as it is on concern for my well-being. Perhaps the time would be better spent reflecting on, for example, Neidenfuhr's exigency thesis."

Mrs. O'Toole shrugged with some hostility.

Anthony calmly mounted the stairs to the house's second floor. He entered his bedroom, audibly closing the door behind him.

Outside his bedroom window there was an old oak tree,

naked, close to death. One of its branches seemed to reach out toward Anthony.

Anthony reflected on Neidenfuhr's exigency thesis and giggled. He didn't wonder at it this time; indeed, Anthony took some delight in his giggle, drawing air savagely, turning himself a bright crimson.

For warmth he piled on two shirts and three sweaters, his overcoat held a hostage on a hook by the front door. The only available footwear was slippers, not at all appropriate, although Anthony felt he could make do.

Anthony propped the bedroom window open with a sliderule and gingerly poked his head through. He glanced downwards, calculating the height and the maximum velocity he'd achieve should he happen to lose his purchase, and Anthony was satisfied that barring some integrant he was not factoring in (could the sheer weight of his intellect cause him to plummet head-first?) this eventuality would not prove lethal.

The oak tree received him willingly.

Anthony sat in its branches and wondered how exactly one climbs down a tree. He had seen boys do it, but he had never paid attention. For some reason the laws of physics seemed not to apply to little boys in trees, at least, Anthony couldn't whip them into strict obedience. Anthony reached out a slippered toe and daintily made contact with a branch below.

∞   ∞   ∞

Charlene Luttor was refusing to eat her creamed corn. This was a political move; Charlene was quite hungry and creamed corn, while disgusting in theory, didn't actually taste that bad. But it somehow behooved young Charlene to wrinkle her nose and shove her plate away rudely. "This stuff stinks."

Lottie Luttor stared at her daughter blankly, cradling her head on her knuckles.

"Really and truly," Charlene persisted, worried about her mom's vacant state. "It sucks."

That got no reaction whatsoever. Charlene played her trump. "It sucks shit," she mumbled tentatively.

Lottie rolled her eyes suddenly but dreamily. "How's come you told Logan that you hated him?"

Charlene had forgotten she'd done that. Feeling a bit sick inside, she blamed it on the creamed corn. "I don't hate him, actually."

"Actually," said Lottie, "you like him. I know, 'cause I found this underneath the sofa."

Lottie took out a piece of paper on which Charlene had crayoned a drawing. It was a picture of Logan standing in his goal crease. "It sure is good, too. I figured I'd put it up on the fridge."

Charlene blushed deeply. "It's just stupit."

"But what's this?" Lottie stabbed with one of her thick red fingers. "What's that sucker doing there?"

Charlene had depicted Logan with a strange bird-like creature hunched upon his shoulder.

Charlene stared at the beast, unable to remember. "Looks like a bird, except for the like fur and, um, teeth."

"Hey! You wanna go to the hockey game?"

Charlene considered it. Something about going to the hockey game was frightening, but she couldn't figure out what. She finally nodded.

So Lottie grabbed great bulky ski jackets, an enormous one for herself, a tiny one for her daughter, and out they went. Charlene raised her eyes toward the winter sky. Then she frowned, disappointed. "Where's the consolation?"

"Don't you start that," Lottie said mock-sternly. "Lord knows what that's all about." Lottie was struggling to light up a Rothman's in the wind. Charlene wondered why her mother hadn't lit it inside their little house, but she was used to that sort of thing. It took about seven matches. Lottie had turned a brilliant red from all the huffing and puffing. "Things in the sky," Lottie said, "is all I know."

Charlene took another peek—there wasn't anything in the sky but a bunch of stars. She opened her mouth and began to sing a plaintive ballad about a woman who's husband was hanged beneath the full moon.

∞   ∞   ∞

The first time Charlene Luttor had seen Logan, she'd woken up and wandered into the livingroom, eager to watch "Captain Kangaroo." She was surprised to find the television already on, the Captain being watched by an enormous man wearing only his underwear. This man turned and said, " 'Captain Kangaroo.' My favourite."

Charlene was too surprised to do anything but nod.

"Actually," the man wearing only his underwear went on, "Captain Kangaroo himself is not my favourite. That other guy is. Mr. Greenjeans. But I haven't seen him yet this morning."

"He died," Charlene informed him bluntly.

The huge man wearing only his underwear began to cry. He cried softly and gently, and then it was over so quickly that Charlene wasn't sure it had actually happened.

"What's your name?" Charlene demanded.

"Logan. What's yours?"

"Charlene Marigold Luttor. Why do you just have *Logan*?"

"It's all I need."

The answer, vague and somehow mocking, irritated Charlene. "I hate Captain Kangaroo," she announced. She jumped off the sofa and went to spin the dial, well aware, as was every citizen of Falconbridge, that Elmore Daisy had shanghaied all the other stations.

"What did he die of?" Logan asked. He had reached a hand

inside his underwear and was scratching at something leisurely.

"Who?" snapped Charlene.

"Mr. Greenjeans."

"He died of from being an old man."

Charlene turned off the television and ignored the huge man wearing only his underwear.

The next day he was back in the same place, same underwear, staring at "Captain Kangaroo." He didn't look too good. His eyes were red and watery. Something softened inside Charlene. She went over to place a hand on his knee.

It was just about the ugliest knee she'd ever seen. It reminded Charlene of the marble bags that the schoolboys toted, except that it wasn't made out of purple velveteen, it was dead skin. Charlene saw that the partner knee was, if anything, uglier. Charlene put her hand on the man's shoulder instead.

"He was an old man, so he died," she said. "That's all."

"Yeah," nodded Logan. "Yeah."

∞   ∞   ∞

The crowd at the Falconbridge Coliseum was somewhere between three and four thousand people. They all expected to watch one or two periods of shinny, and then they expected someone to score. There was some heavy wagering going on, particularly among the press people. Ridout to win was paying 2–1, while Logan was up around 7–1. Quite a few people were betting on Logan, although the heavy-drinking square woman, Mickey, was the only one vocal about her preference. "I'm betting on Logan the wanker," she told her cohorts, "because my husband was a wanker, God bless him."

The players were very excited, taking their warm-up circles at a rapid clip, bumping elbows, no one saying a word.

Logan prepared his crease meticulously, at least he pretended to. The Coliseum ice was never that good, so Logan thought that cleaning up was more or less in vain. Mostly he was doing it because Bram Ridout was doing it. Ridout held his violently coloured mask in the crook of his arm, the three eyes glowering at Logan. The kid's shoulders and head jerked convulsively, and he seemed to have developed a new tic, a quick and irregular blinking. Ridout's eyes would flash on and off, five times a second, and then bulge open for a long moment.

Ridout was not a picture of health, mental or physical. His skin was a strange colour, marbled with reds and yellows.

He wore an expression unique among inhabitants of the third stone from the Sun. It might be described as baffled arrogance or arrogant bafflement.

Some townboys came to the glass near Ridout and reached over with autograph books and pencils. Bram Ridout, after staring at them for an arrogant, baffled moment, swung his stick, shooing them away.

He's cracking, thought Logan, to which his heart answered softly, *You're a fine one to talk.*

Then his heart whispered, *Look over there.*

Kristal Donahue was sitting in the top row of benches away down at the other end. She was staring down at her lap.

A huge, bearded Hope player was suddenly blocking Logan's view of his true love. Logan recognized him as the defenceman who had rendered yesterday's open-ice body-check against Jay Fineweather. Jay had done a triple half-gainer and landed unceremoniously on his butt. The Hope player had grinned broadly, evilly, and that's what he was doing now, his eyes atwinkle. He looked like an elf with a thyroid condition.

This man said to Logan, "Loogan frem Kizzle. Lars Løkan frem Kizzle. Lars fak Kizzle."

"I beg your pardon?" asked Logan, very politely.

This time the Hope defenceman accompanied himself with hand gestures. He thumped Logan on the chest. "Loogan frem Kizzle." He thumped himself on the chest. "Lars frem Kizzle." He put his hands together and pumped them energetically,

101

producing a series of wet, mulching sounds. "Lars fak Kizzle."

Logan nodded. "Yes, well, um, whatever you say."

"Lars fak Kizzle."

"Got it. Lars fak Kizzle."

The bearded man grinned and skated away.

"Lars fak Kizzle," mumbled Logan somewhat absent-mindedly.

Logan remembered that the day was Sunday, and he felt a sharp, pointed sadness poke around inside. Logan wasn't looking forward to an evening of sobriety. Logan desperately didn't want to lose the game. This wasn't just the presence of all the spectators—they'd booed him before, lustily and with conviction—nor was it the newspaper reporters. Logan knew they were for the most part from small-town papers, the Clipperton *Courier*, the Hope *Herald*. It wasn't even as simple as fear of banishment to South Grouse, although the memory of the hospital, shadowed in the grey dawn, certainly did Logan's spirit no good.

Logan couldn't have said why the game had suddenly acquired such significance. We know it was because the hole in Logan's heart was the size of a hockey puck.

He hadn't acquired the hole in any of the usual ways. Logan had never been married, there was no tragic love affair, no ginger-haired children unwillingly abandoned with tiny teardrops streaking their cheeks. Dr. Bermondsey could probably give you an idea of how the hole came to be, but first he'd have to light his pipe, something he was unable to do, and he'd use long words, vague expressions, case histories from the fifteenth century.

You would grow impatient with Dr. Bermondsey. Everybody does. You'd wave your hands in the air and say, "Look, are you saying that Logan is crazy?"

Dr. Bermondsey would strike a match, hover it over the cold ashes in the pipebowl. "Emphatically not so."

∞   ∞   ∞

As soon as Kenny Pringle dropped the puck for the opening face-off, Jean-Guy Cabot grabbed one of the Hope players and punched out most of his teeth. The huge bearded Hope player took out after Jean-Guy, only to be intercepted by Faron Quinn, all six-foot-five of him. Soon every player had a partner. Some were merely holding each other like ballroom dancers. Other couples were more actively grappling, some were causing blood and bicuspids to rain onto the ice.

Bram Ridout took a few long strides from his net and seemed to be beckoning Logan with a series of head jerks. Logan carefully laid his stick on the ice and skated down toward him.

As he drew near, Ridout lashed out savagely with a right cross. Logan watched the fist sail by.

"What the fuck are you doing?" demanded Logan.

"Come on. Fight!" snarled Bram. He took another punch, this one a weak left that Logan merely wiped aside.

"Fucking *kid*," muttered Logan.

"You're gonna lose!" taunted Ridout musically. Logan noticed that Bram's speaking voice was high and squeaky. His *s* sound was thick and silly, almost a lisp. The kid tried to land another punch, his fist deflecting painfully off Logan's shoulder pad.

"Hey, you better watch that," said Logan. "That's your glove hand."

Bram Ridout stopped abruptly. The kid stared at Logan with his look of arrogant bafflement and then stated matter-of-factly, "I got the best glove hand in the *world*." This seemed to be news to Ridout himself. The very voicing of it made him step backwards suddenly as if startled.

"It's good," agreed Logan.

"In the whole wide *world*!"

"Yeah, right." Logan turned away. "I'm going back down there now, kid."

"Hey!" shouted Bram Ridout, turning Logan around. "Remember Marshall Instant Pudding?"

It was certainly an unexpected question, but Logan did indeed remember Marshall Instant Pudding. In his first years in the National Hockey League, Marshall Foods Inc. ran a promotional campaign whereby every box of pudding contained a plastic coin that pictured a hockey player.

Bram Ridout nodded—it looked like someone had his head on a string and was yanking it up and down. "I ate Marshall Instant Pudding," said the kid. "I must have gone through three or four boxes a day. I hated it. Couldn't fucking stand it. But I wanted the coins. I wanted all of the coins. I wanted Sawchuk and Bower and Beliveau and Mahovlich and Esposito and Orr. But who did I keep getting? *You.* Every goddamn box I ate, out comes another coin with fucking Logan on it. You know what you can do with a Logan Marshall Instant Pudding Coin? Sweet dick-all. You could maybe trade fifteen Logans for a piece of dog turd."

Logan wondered if that were an established exchange rate.

"You shouldn't drink," Ridout continued. "You wasted your talents and you're a bum. Fuck off back down to the other end and wait for the puck to go by you. I'm not about to let it in."

Ridout turned away, his shoulders jerking unevenly like an antique steam engine.

Bram Ridout was at the end of a very long line of people who had called Logan a drunken bum with wasted talents. Logan usually dismissed these comments casually, but something in Ridout's snarling tone stung.

Logan glanced up at Kristal Donahue. She was staring down at him very sadly indeed.

Sirens went off inside Logan. Red alert.

Logan mumbled bitterly, "*Lars fak Kizzle.*"

Twelve

Joe Fineweather's Vision and its ensuing state were widely misinterpreted as advanced drunkenness. We can't blame the townspeople for this—Joe did come down Lowell Avenue ricocheting off walls, fair lathering at the mouth. He seemed incapable of speech, although he flapped his gums and lolled his tongue. The one word he did manage to get out—after a series of moans and blubbers—was "Hellzapoppin'!"

Uncle Joe had a tough time gathering his thoughts, but once he did, on top of the pile was how to get by Carl Luttor. After all, that man had refused him admission on the last occasion, when Joe had had the requisite five bucks. As he neared the Coliseum, Joe decided to try some mystical, magical stuff. At the entrance Joe closed his eyes and prayed to his many deities, and as he reached the turnstile, Joe Fineweather was invisible to the eyes of men.

Except Carl Luttor grabbed him anyway. "You can't come in here!" Carl said haughtily. "There are decent people in here. My granddaughter's here!"

"Carl," said Joe reasonably, "I don't have time to argue with you. Logan needs me."

"Logan needs you, eh?" Logan was no favourite of Carl's. "Well, Logan's playing hockey right now, so I guess he can't need you that bad."

Joe Fineweather knew one more magical trick. He fastened

his uneven eyes on a spot beyond Carl Luttor's left shoulder. He hefted one of his fingers and gesticulated mysteriously. "Hey," he said, "look over there."

It worked. Carl Luttor swung his head around. Joe skipped nimbly through the turnstile.

The Coliseum was even more crowded than it had been two days earlier. Uncle Joe made a mental note to henceforth attend every Falcon home game.

Joe pushed his way through the crowd. The one advantage to being unpopular, reflected Uncle Joe, is that people have as little to do with you as possible. Quite a few men swung around angrily as he pushed them aside, but when they saw it was just Old Joe Fineweather they scowled and turned away.

They were more interested in the fight, anyway, thought Joe disdainfully. Gloves and helmets strewn about the ice, the players on top of each other, pounding with all their might.

The good thing was that, because of the fight, no one was paying much attention to Logan. Logan stood near centre ice, and as far as anyone could tell, not doing a thing. Joe Fineweather knew better. He knew that Logan's brain was forming a bucket brigade and that any moment tears were going to come flaming out of Logan. Joe knew that Logan's stomach was doing clumsy acrobatics, borrowing things from its neighbour to throw up. And Joe Fineweather knew that Logan's heart had, like a dwarf white star, collapsed upon itself to form a black hole. Yahoo had flown the coop. Joe knew all this, but none of the particulars. Wisdom informed him that it had to do with that pit-holed muddy area that lies between true hearts and sweaty bodies.

Joe pounded on the Plexiglas. "Logan!" he bellowed, but the sound was lost in the roar. "Hey, Logan!" Joe recalled that Boyd Boyce was sitting on a high stool just around the corner. He found that man sitting placidly, his finger on the red button, ever vigilant, waiting for someone to score a goal.

"Hello, Boyd Boyce!"

Boyd nodded in an official manner. Joe picked up the back of

the stool and dumped Boyd Boyce. He stepped up and grabbed
the top of the glass. Joe Fineweather felt people grabbing hold
of his trouser legs, but he shook them free. And then he flipped
over, delighted with his own agility, and found himself in the
rink proper.

He immediately fell down, his Hushpuppies being woefully
inadequate for the glacial terrain. Joe surveyed the painted
lines and boxes and circles. Joe Fineweather decided, in deference to both his shoes and an undeniable amount of grog-
addle, to crawl over to Logan.

He reached him just as Logan was about to blow. Logan had
been existing in a state of numbness, but his faculties had
rallied splendidly and were prepared to go berserk, to par-
ticulate in a grizzly way. Logan opened his mouth (intending to issue forth a scream that would shame Koko into
retirement) when he felt someone tug his hockey socks down
to his ankles.

Logan looked iceward and found Uncle Joe Fineweather
grinning at him.

"Logan," Joe said, "pull up your socks."

∞   ∞   ∞

It was the most bizarre hockey game Kristal had ever seen,
except that nobody had played any hockey so far. Kristal
looked down from the bleachers and watched as one lover
(Løkan) systematically demolished the players on her home
town team. Another lover (Logan) stood in the middle of the
rink, becoming uncorked. Life had its thumbs working; that
cork was a fraction away from blasting into the ceiling.

Kristal watched, incredulously, as Joe Fineweather appeared
and crawled over to Logan on hands and knees. Joe tugged
down Logan's socks.

Joe spoke to Logan.

Logan laughed.

He laughed and to Kristal Donahue it rang magically. It

107

sounded like Logan had a spacepod somewhere about to get blasted to smithereens by some very serious mindfuckers.

Kristal smacked her fist into the palm of her other hand. "Go get 'em, Mars," she whispered happily.

∞   ∞   ∞

By the time all the penalties had been assigned, the greater part of both teams was packed tightly into the sin bin. For about ten minutes both teams would play with three skaters a side, and at the end of that time the Hope Blazers would get an additional skater for a little more than three minutes.

Logan refused to think about those three minutes; for now he worried about the first ten.

Big George Tyack had cunningly removed Jay Fineweather a moment or two before the fighting stopped, and the ploy worked in that Kenny Pringle allowed Jay to continue playing. Vic Pheresford likewise went unpunished; although he did fight, and savagely, Pringle took pity on him for getting beaten up so badly. So there were two very good offensive players available to the Falcons. The defence, however, was crippled. All four players went to the box, although Parker Mackie's sentence of four minutes was less than half the others'.

∞   ∞   ∞

At first, Anthony O'Toole felt massive disdain for the woman seated beside him. She was partisan in the most irrational way. Any time the puck drifted near (within a spatial co-ordinate that Anthony could equate both with speed and time, and then, by factoring out the space — with an inverse topology — arrive at an actual temporal co-ordinate, which was Nobel Prize-winning stuff) Logan's net, the woman would squeeze her hands together until the knuckles blanched. If the play should move down into the Hope end (the implications would have been mind-boggling, except that little Anthony's mind was unbogglable) the woman would lose interest, she'd pick at a mustard stain on her jeans. Anthony wanted (vaguely) to comfort the woman, especially as the next three minutes were going to prove very rough. Logan had survived the previous ten heroically, but the Hope Blazers were about to ice an additional man. (The player was standing in the penalty box, eyes riveted up at the clock.) With four skaters to three, it seemed unlikely that Mr. Logan could keep the puck out of the net.

When the man from Hope jumped on the ice, everyone in the stands fell silent. The lady beside Anthony said a word softly, a word that he'd never encountered before but could prove statistically was vulgar.

The Falcons had only one defenceman, the flamboyant but often hapless Mackie. The other three sat forlornly in the penalty box. Jay Fineweather could play well as a backender, but he was exhausted, having spent eight of the last ten minutes trying to win the game for the Falcons. All in all, Anthony thought, Mr. Logan doesn't stand a chance.

The Hope Blazers came down the ice. Parker Mackie tried one of his patented sprawling checks, with the usual result—he went sailing by the puck-carrier. Hope had three men in the clear, and they passed the puck back and forth almost playfully. Logan stood there, crouched and wary, depending on his instincts. The shot came in a nanosecond, the Hope centreman cranking up and blasting. It was a perfect shot, cruising about six inches off the ice and heading for the corner.

Logan did the splits, and the toe of his skate arrived just in time to deflect the puck upwards and away from the net. His teammate Stanley Huculak swung at the puck in desperation and connected. The puck threaded its way through Hope players and rolled up-ice.

Logan was still doing the splits. Anthony noted that Mr. Logan was seemingly unable to get up. Anthony did the cognitive equivalent of tearing up his notes. This, he thought, is it.

109

The Hope Blazers started back.

Logan reached overhead and grabbed the crossbar with both hands, leaving his stick on the ice. Logan pulled himself up. A Hope player shot. Logan's legs buckled and he crumpled to the ice. The shot came, a high hard one, and just as it was about to enter the net Logan threw his blocker up into the air. Logan got enough of the puck to send it circling away and it leapt over the glass and into the stands. Kenny Pringle blew his whistle.

There was no applause for Logan, not that he didn't deserve it. It just seemed silly to clap for the crumpled pile of humanity that lay in the goal crease.

Jay Fineweather was the first to him, kneeling down and finding Logan's head pretty much where it was supposed to be. Then George Tyack came leaping over the boards, slipping frantically in his street shoes. Soon the whole team was clustered around, blocking Logan from sight.

"I'm confident he will be all right," said little Anthony to the woman beside, amazed at the words coming out of his mouth. In truth, Anthony O'Toole suspected that Logan now possessed non-legs, antipods.

At the other end of the ice, Bram Ridout was going through histics and spasms. This time he added to the repertoire some arm movements, his elbows flying upwards simultaneously.

The woman beside little Anthony suddenly stood bolt upright and shouted, "Mars! Logan! Get up!"

The people seated behind Logan's net started to clap. Anthony O'Toole's heart quickened, getting more exercise than it ever had in its life. The applause spread and when it had filled the Coliseum the Falconbridge Falcons skated away from the net.

Logan assumed his stance.

DAY FOUR

Thirteen

A photographer from the Gormsley *Globe* took a picture of Logan as he was tumbling to the ice. It showed with amazing clarity Logan's face, his mouth a tortured, twisted grimace. Logan's eyes had a distinct madness about them, a black burning. The photographer captured the instant when the puck bounced off Logan's blocker. His arm was stretched to such an extent that one would it think it had popped out of the socket. This photograph was so good that the man was able to sell it to the big dailies in Montreal and Toronto.

The story itself was only somewhat noteworthy. Two teams in an obscure hockey league had battled through fifteen periods of hockey (twelve overtime) and the game was still undecided. Without the photograph it is unlikely anyone would have cared.

At about ten o'clock on Monday morning, Elmore Daisy received a phone call. It made him giggle insanely. He had put Falconbridge on the map.

"Hockey Night in Canada" was coming.

∞　　　∞　　　∞

Logan awoke and felt possessed of screaming banshees and whirling dervishes. He stumbled out of bed (his *own* bed, some part of his mind registered, an old, stained box spring, a sheet

113

that resembled the Shroud of Turin) and bounced off the walls towards the bathroom. Logan clutched his head and groaned.

Logan threw the bathroom door open. As soon as he stepped inside he realized he wasn't hung over. All the moaning, clutching and stumbling had been force of habit. Logan actually felt pretty good. Logan was adaptable. He dropped to the floor and began to do push-ups. He did about fifteen and then collapsed. The cold floor felt nice beneath his long naked body.

Logan cocked an eye toward the window. Through the glass he saw an angry sky; the clouds collided and churned toward Heaven. Logan shut his eye. "Big storm coming," Logan muttered conversationally, "only Darla doesn't know a thing about it." Darla had again been featured in Logan's dreams, again she'd paraded about in the buffbare before a weather map, only the map pictured strange lands and the names were written in a script that seemed not of this world. It was the nakedness that Logan remembered best. His little buddy the hard-on rushed to the scene, found himself squashed against freezing bathroom tiles and fled.

"What time is it anyway?" Logan demanded aloud. "Hope it's not late." He pulled himself up, stood near the toilet and urinated nonchalantly, his hands buckled at his waist, aiming the stream with broad movements of his hips. As he pissed, Logan stared down at his knees. "Filthy Sirian mindfuckers," he snarled. His left knee tossed out a little jolt of pain; Logan thought it best to ignore it.

Logan reached up to feel his jaw. He knew he needed a shave, but he suspected his beard might be too thick for his razor, a disposable that Logan had held onto for years. His fingers brushed against his left cheek, and Logan roared with pain. Then he remembered the fight, and went to the mirror to look.

The cut on his cheek had taken about thirteen stitches, some inside, some out. Logan saw, not without a trace of glee, that the cut would leave him with a pirate's scar, cruel and violent. Logan also noted that his eyes were black, purple and puffy, and the right half of his lower lip was swollen and caked with blood.

The fight had been with Løkan. Sometime in the twelfth period of overtime, Løkan had parked himself in front of Logan's crease. Logan took his stick and banged it against the man's ankles a couple of times, just a suggestion that he stand elsewhere and also fak Kizzle no more. Without warning Lars shot the butt-end of his stick into Logan's stomach, knocking his wind into the front-row seats. Logan tumbled and Løkan went with him. From that point on it was a simple, though brutal, fight. Logan, smaller, stunned and breathless, got the worst of it.

The only good thing about it was that Kenny Pringle judged in Logan's favour, handing out a five-minute major to Løkan, giving Logan a two-minute minor. That gave the Falcons a man advantage for three minutes, which was all well and good except Bram Ridout wasn't biting. They never came close to scoring on him.

Logan didn't know where the kid got his energy. At times Logan suspected vast quantities of drugs (this also explained the ever-increasing tics and mannerisms) but at other times he flirted with the notion of black magic. Logan believed in black magic in a non-specific way. He had seen a great but warped power twist minds and bodies, he had seen mangled people littered about the lawn. And he suspected Ridout of communing with this evil thing. Moreover, there was something very strange about that Fiberglas mask. It played tricks; sometimes Logan couldn't tell which of the three eyes was painted. The forks of lightning seemed to change position, as if a storm were taking place upon the blood-red shield.

The weirdest thing about the kid was the way he played. If a seventeenth-century witch-hunter from Massachusetts ever got a look at him, Ridout would be dipped and fried, no questions asked. Often it looked like the kid was doing a

115

cheerful and graceful little dance, and it was coincidental that pucks kept bouncing off his limbs. Ridout had also come up with the odd superhuman act, jumping twelve feet from a standing position (in skates, no less) to smother a puck. And, as the kid himself maintained, it was possible that his glove hand was the best in the world. This, thought Logan grimly, was no credit to Bram Ridout, because his glove hand was as alien as Logan's knees. That was the only explanation. The glove hand would fly toward an airborne puck before Ridout could have spied it, before the firing of a single synapse. The glove hand kept playing regardless of the position or state the rest of the kid was in, completely autonomous. It was, Logan strongly suspected, a mindfucker from the Dogstar Sirius.

∞   ∞   ∞

When the horn went at the end of the twelfth overtime, Pringle called the two captains together and requested yet another recess until the following evening. It was very late, Kenny explained, and he had to drive thirty miles, go to bed, and be up at six for his job in the mines.

In the dressingroom, Coach Tyack had assembled the Falconbridge Falcons in a circle around him. He knelt in their midst holding three golden coins. "Here he is now," whispered Big George to the other players.

Logan tried to ignore them all. He walked over to his stall and started throwing equipment into it.

Big George held up the coins. One side pictured a strange creature, half man, half bird. On the other side was a woman, draped in an Olympian goddess's gown. "I Ching time!" called Big George. "Works every time."

Logan farted foully.

"Come on, Logan, old buddy," pleaded George Tyack. "All you have to do is toss the coins. I'll handle the rest." Big George jangled the coins in his huge hand, demonstrating how much fun it could be.

"Oh, all right." Logan went to the centre of the circle and squatted, except his knees conspired to give out altogether, dumping him on his keester. He received the three golden coins from Big George.

"We need to ask the question," said Big George.

"How about," suggested Logan, "where can you get a drink in Falconbridge on a Sunday night?"

The Falcons indicated by a soft grumbling that they didn't care much for Logan's flippant disdain.

"The question is," said Big George, "will Logan win the hockey game?"

"The question is," suggested Jay Fineweather, "what gives?"

"Fair enough," said Logan, looking hard at his friend. "What gives?" Logan launched the coins. They spun for a long moment before being still. They all showed the same side up, the ancient bird-god.

George Tyack drew a broken line on a piece of toilet paper:

—— ——

"Hey!" Logan was impressed with his roll. "A buck says I can do it again," he said. "Three birdy-goombas."

"Just throw them," said someone harshly.

Logan did. Three bird-gods.

Big George drew another broken line.

"I can do it *again*! Now do I have any takers? Three birdies, one buck." He looked around the circle. Jean-Guy Cabot nodded at him. Logan rattled the coins in his hand for a few seconds. "Come on, birdman! Come on now, birdy-baby!" Logan released the coins suddenly. Three more bird-gods. "All right!" shouted Logan.

The coach worked carefully, inscribing a third divided line.

"This is foolhardy," said Logan, "but I'm riding something

117

here. I'm riding a big cosmo-wave, I'm hanging ten, and I'm saying that for two bucks that birdman gonna come land on Logey's shoulders three times."

Jean-Guy grunted. Vic Pheresford and Norm Huffman winked.

Logan threw the coins. "The birdman, uh, uh, uhh!"

Big George, busy working on his sheet of toilet paper, which now looked like this:

muttered, "Horus."

"Huh?"

"Not *birdman*," Big George explained. "Horus."

"Horace, baby!" screamed Logan. He held the coins to his ears. "What did you say, Horace? No, I don't think—really? I don't know if we should. What? Okay, then." He addressed the team. "Horace says that for a fin he will come back three times. He's my little Horace buddy-baby!" Logan kissed the coins.

All fifteen of the Falcons nodded at Logan. Even Big George, concerned and troubled by the diagram on the toilet paper, said, "I'll take a piece of that action."

Logan turned the coins over and looked at the goddess pictured there. "No, darling," he cooed, "I don't want you at all, at all. I just want my little buddy Horace." Logan rattled the coins. He rattled them for almost a full minute. Then, furiously, he launched them into the air.

Three ladies.

"Bitch!" Logan shouted.

Big George added a solid, unbroken line to his drawing:

Petulantly, Logan made his final throw. Horus/Horace, the birdman, smiled at him three times.

"Too late, you manky scumbag."

George Tyack's completed hexagram looked like this:

He consulted the I Ching.

" 'Pi,' " he read. " 'But let the party re-examine itself, as if by divination, whether his virtue be great, unintermitting and firm. If it be so, there will be no error.' " Big George appraised the information. "That sounds okay to me."

"Read some more," urged Jay Fineweather.

Big George pointed to the bottom line and consulted the massive volume in his hands. " 'Let the breast be full of sincerity as an earthenware vessel is of its contents, and in the end it will bring other advantages.' " Big George's finger moved upwards to the next broken line. " 'We see the movement toward union and attachment proceeding from the inward. With firm correctness there will be good fortune.' "

Logan was still fuming at the ancient god Horace. He paid no attention.

"Uh-oh," said Big George, his finger arriving at the third divided line. " 'We see the subject seeking for union with such as ought not to be associated with.' " With the next line, Coach Tyack looked happier. " 'We see the subject searching for union with the one beyond himself. With firm correctness there will be good fortune.' "

"Firm correctness," repeated Jay.

" 'The fifth line, undivided,' " read Big George, " 'affords the most illustrious instance of seeking union and attachment. We see the King urging his pursuit of the game in three directions, and allowing the escape of all the beasts before him, while the people of his towns do not warn one another to prevent it. There will be good fortune.' Goody-goody," said Big George. "And the last one," he continued, still buoyed by the happy prophecy before. " 'We see one seeking union and attachment without having taken the first step to such an end.' " Big George's grin vanished abruptly. " 'There will be evil.' "

The Falconbridge Falcons turned to stare at Logan sullenly.

"All this I Ching stuff is for the birds," said that man. "I know what's going on."

"What?" asked George Tyack.

Logan pulled the coach into one of the dressingroom's corners. "You know about my knees, right?" For a clue as to his reference, Logan gesticulated upwards in the general direction of the Dogstar Sirius. Big George turned his head toward Heaven and then nodded. "Don't tell the other guys," he whispered, winking conspiratorially.

"Right," nodded Logan. He put his arm around Big George's shoulders and pulled him closer. "The thing about it is," Logan said, "I figure Ridout's glove hand is from the same damn place."

Logan never knew why he did things like that. Big George gasped and turned beet-red. He had to clutch at his heart with a giant hand. "Goodness gracious," the coach moaned. "It's happening, just like Quodmon said it would."

Percy St.J. Quodmon was the loon who'd written *The Dogstar* (Dogstar Publishing, 1955). His theory that the inhabitants were not corporate upon the Dogstar. They could occupy bodies or parts thereof on other planets, and they took advantage of this to wage war and settle disputes among themselves. This nut Quodmon had predicted that a large-scale Sirian civil war would be fought upon our little blue stone in a winter during the nineteen-seventies, and Coach Tyack figured this was it: Ridout's glove hand *vs.* Logan's knees.

"Logan," said the coach, calming now but still dangerously excited, "you better come home with me."

∞   ∞   ∞

Coach George Tyack lived close by the arena in a tiny bungalow that he'd built himself. The house was perfect, a dainty quaint thing that seemed like a picture torn out of a storybook. It was hard to believe that Big George had rendered it with his huge beefy hams.

The inside of the tiny house was the same, filled with lovely and fragile things, all the handiwork of George Tyack. Big George made model sailing ships and wood-carvings of ducks, which he sat gingerly on handmade doilied tabletops. His walls were covered with batiks, macramé and slightly pornographic needlework. Several watercolours boasted stark Ontario landscapes, the world a wash of whites. The signature in the corner was modest and simple:

G. Tyack

All this applies to every room in the house with the exception of the den. It was the den, the biggest room, that housed George's incredible library. The walls were solid with books, tightly packed, and books overflowed the shelves, they rose from the ground, they leaned drunkenly against walls and in the corners.

Logan ran into the den as soon as he entered the house. He selected a book at random, a slender and elegant volume entitled *Why I Had To*. The author's name was Harriet Rollins. Logan snapped the book open, impatient to find out just exactly what Harriet Rollins had to do, and why.

Big George Tyack went to his kitchen and poured out two tumblers' worth of fairly decent rye. He came back looking distressed. Big George absent-mindedly handed a drink to Logan, who accepted it absent-mindedly. Then the coach went to a bookshelf and pulled down Prof. Quodmon's lifework, *The Dogstar*.

Harriet Rollins, Logan was learning, had to do a lot of things. When she was seven, she had to take off all of her clothes in front of her stepfather, who would then render her likeness in butter. When the likeness was completed, the stepfather would attack the dairy-product effigy and force Harriet to watch. Logan didn't see why she had to do that.

"I think," Big George spoke up, "it might have something to do with the equinox and the associated parallaxes and all such like. To wit, if the so-called dog days occur in high summer, it makes sense that there be some correspond, a negative expression of same, in the winter. Does that make any sense to you?"

Compared to some of the things the coach said within the safe confines of his bungalow, it made a lot of sense, but Logan merely grunted, concentrating on *Why I Had To*. Harriet, at twelve years of age, now had to live with an even stranger stepfather. This one, monomaniacal about personal hygiene, was naked all day long, licking himself clean as a cat would, forcing Harriet to assist on the hard-to-reach places. Logan was getting angry.

"Contrariwise," persisted Big George Tyack, "the annuality factor may be a mere bagatelle! Perhaps they simply commute at will." The coach frowned at this frightening hypothesis.

Logan was dreading reading about the day that Harriet started sprouting breasts and hips if she went through this much shit before. Chapter Three began: "My maker endowed me well in the motherly glands."

Oh, Christ, she's even got big ones, Logan thought sadly.

"Do you want another drinky-poo, Logey?" asked Big George. The coach had a little drinking problem himself, had had it ever since he checked a man cleanly into the boards and killed the poor sod, which is why the coach said *drinky-poo*.

Logan, his eyes racing back and forth, merely nodded and stuck out his empty glass.

Harriet now had to do a lot of weird things, with a lot of weird people. These things were so damn weird that they had never even occurred to Logan, and he was the one who had once convinced a girl to perform oral sex on him while he did an imitation of the evangelist faith-healer Ernest Angley.

George Tyack came back with the drinky-poos. Caught up in his own thoughts, he didn't notice that as Logan finished reading one page he would tear it out of the book and crumple it.

Big George had his own problems, namely, how to deal with these alien mindfuckers. The certainty of intelligent non-corporeal life on the Dogstar Sirius (and earthly contact with) was documented beyond question. For example, Professor Quodmon points out in the Introduction, the Dogstar Sirius is worshipped by the Dogon tribe in Africa. They also worship, and have for centuries, Sirius's tiny companion star. The point being, this companion star was only discovered by Western astronomers at the turn of this century, and was not actually *seen* until we started developing really powerful telescopes in the fifties. So how did the Dogons know it was there? Ask any Dogon.

"They came and told us," the Dogon will reply matter-of-factly.

Logan was reading:

Next I had to pull down his trousers with my teeth. His erect manly thing poked me hurtfully in the eyeball. I had to take his manhood into my mouth. Above, he started to gesticulate. "Bayuh-bee! Bayuh-bee!" he sang out, in imitation of the well-known Christian broadcaster, Ernest

It didn't really say that. Logan was afraid that it might say that, or maybe he was even hoping that it would. Logan deserved it.

If you search through mythology, you will note a startling similarity concerning otherworldly visitations. All the males are tiny and green. Mescal, the god of peyote, is a little green guy, and leprechauns are little and dress in green, and certainly those little green men from outer space are little and green. The women, however, are larger and luminescent and invariably hover in the sky. The Blessed Virgin Mary that appeared at

Fatima was described that way. And doesn't the Good Witch of the North travel in a floating silver bubble? (Harriet, at twenty-eight years of age, began to receive visitations from an otherworldly woman who, consistent with the above hypothesis, arrived encased in a glowing silver cocoon and hovered about a foot off the ground. This otherworldly woman told Harriet that she didn't have to do all those things. There was only one thing she had to do.) How do we account for these remarkable similarities that span generations, religions and races? Very simply, according to Prof. Quodmon.

"Mindfuckers from the Dogstar Sirius," gasped Logan, because it looked like that's who Harriet Rollins was becoming involved with.

George Tyack slammed a fist into his palm. "But how do we fight them?"

Then Logan found out exactly what Harriet had to do. It was what sent her to the mental hospital (the one in South Grouse, coincidentally) where she wrote the book *Why I Had To*. What she had to do was take a straight razor and chop off some poor guy's dick. A silver lady floating in the air told her that she had to.

Logan's stomach shrivelled. His alien knees shook, realizing that Earthlings were far more dangerous than they'd thought. Logan's hard-on packed his bags and went to New Zealand.

"What do we do?" asked Big George again.

His hand trembling, Logan slipped *Why I Had To* back into the almost non-existent gap it had left among the books. He finished his drink in one long pull. "Got to go," he told Big George. The coach was thinking hard about the Sirius mindfuckers. He nodded and Logan left.

Clouds covered the sky; there were no constellations there.

∞   ∞   ∞

Logan went to his apartment above the shoe repair shop. He

turned on his television. He was able to watch the last five minutes of a western and then two priests came on television to discuss the New Morality.

Logan was of the opinion that God didn't do such a crackerjack job that He couldn't have worked through Sunday. In fact, how could He have even considered resting, considering His recent creation of the severely twistable mankind?

Logan's mind went off on a bizarre little romp, peeking through doors into padded rooms. Logan climbed into bed before his mind got lost completely.

Logan's sleep was not the sleep of the pure. His mind entertained him with a series of surrealistic films, odd little entries influenced by the German cinema of the twenties.

Logan woke up and felt possessed of screaming banshees and whirling dervishes.

He went to his bathroom and examined his face, which had been beaten up nicely the night before. But, heh-heh, Lars the accursed Kizzle fakir was no raving beauty himself. Because of the gash on his cheek, Logan had to forgo shaving. His growth of four days was grey and scuzzy, and together with the stitches, swollen lip and black eye, Logan looked like someone he wouldn't want to know. Logan had yet to put in his teeth, so he grinned at himself in the mirror, savouring the full effect. Logan was monumentally ugly. Anyone can become a little messy-looking, Logan reasoned, but it takes work to achieve this! Logan's reflection grinned back like a circus geek.

Logan made himself a cup of coffee. He turned on his television and watched "Captain Kangaroo." He mourned Mr. Greenjeans.

Fourteen

Li's Hardware & Furniture was owned and operated by Luk Sun Li.

Li was a very old Chinese dwarf. He may not have qualified officially as a dwarf, but he was without doubt the tiniest man Logan had ever encountered. Li was, Logan estimated, one hundred and forty-seven years old. His face was an area of maybe six square inches that contained well over ten thousand wrinkles. Luk Sun Li had a beard made up of one hair. The hair started in the middle of Li's prune-like chin and fell to his feet. Li dressed ornately, in robes that would have been long and flowing were it not for Li's being a dwarf.

When Logan stepped into the store, Li floated up to him. That was another thing about Li—he seemed always to be suspended a couple of inches off the ground.

"Logan," said Luk Sun Li, "you are a famous and illustrious man!" Li had only been in the country for about seven years, but his English was very good. Li did have trouble with a few words and sounds. Logan had once mischievously taken something out of a box and exclaimed, "What a lollapalooza!" He let it be known by his manner that this was what Canadians said when they took something out of a box. The next time Luk Sun Li de-boxed an article he held it in the air proudly and shouted something so strange that Logan was surprised when Li didn't go "Poof!" and disappear.

"What do you mean, famous?"

By way of answer Li displayed for Logan a copy of the national edition of the *Globe and Mail*. On the front page of the section titled SPORTS was the photograph of Logan.

"Huh!" Logan took the paper and searched for the accompanying story. There wasn't one, other than the three or four lines that captioned the photo. Still, Logan's name was mentioned, M. Logan.

Li waved his little hands philosophically. "Very, very famous," he stated. "Now you're too good a man to work for Li!" Li laughed at his little joke, a sound like a two-inch saw cutting wood. "I shall change the name to Logan's Hardware," he continued in this jocular vein. "That will attract the tourist trade."

"It's just in there because it's a pretty good picture," said Logan, although he would have been hurt to learn how accurate his assessment was.

"I was in attendance on all three days," Li said. Luk Sun Li always came to the Falcons' games, although Logan rarely spotted him. "You played very well, Logan my friend. But, I hasten to add, so does the boy."

"The fucking kid," snarled Logan.

"Quite so," said Li. "The fokking kid. This is his nickname?"

"Right."

"He is quite exceptional, this fokking kid. The fokking kid plays in peace. Logan does not. Logan plays in anger. Who, then, shall win?" Li giggled. Every sentence that ended with a question mark was audibly punctuated by a giggle of long or short duration.

"Peace, hell!" protested Logan. "He tried to take my goddamn head off!"

"Ah!" Luk Sun Li pointed a finger, so small that Logan had to squint to see it. "To the peaceful of spirit, anger is a tool. But anger is your master."

The door to the store opened and a little boy walked in, a

very strangely dressed little boy. Underneath a ski jacket he appeared to be wearing a three-piece suit. His feet were shoved into Oxfords and the Oxfords were shoved into rubber galoshes. Logan recalled his schooldays and thought that this kid must suffer a tremendous amount of abuse for his sartorial transgressions. He'd have been better off if he wore dresses.

"Can I help you?" asked Logan, for that was his job. Luk Sun Li stocked the shelves, made the furniture and pretended he was possessed of ancient wisdom.

"No thank you, sir," said the oddly dressed little boy. "I am but perusing."

"Nice to meet you, But."

The strangely dressed little boy suddenly looked very perplexed. "I beg your pardon?"

"I said nice to meet you, But."

"You have confused a phrase I used to indicate that there was no specific article of which I was in want with my appelation."

"Shouldn't you be in school?" demanded Logan, his stock question to people under sixteen years of age.

"No. I have, in fact, already been awarded my degree. I should be working, it's true, but I decided to take a, um, holiday."

"Oh, yeah. You having fun?"

"This is what I'm endeavouring to determine. I'm not at all sure what to do."

"Well, if you want, But, I can chase you out of the store."

"Is that fun?"

"Is that fun? You gotta be kidding! Christ, that's some of the biggest fun going. Some of my fondest childhood memories involve getting chased out of stores."

"Very well," agreed little Anthony.

Logan pulled himself forward on his stool. "You about ready?"

Little Anthony nodded.

"You sure? This all happens fast, you got to be on the ball."

"I am ready, sir!"

Logan shot out at the strangely dressed little boy. "Hey, you!" he shouted. "Get the hell out of here!"

Anthony O'Toole turned and bolted through the front door. Logan could hear a strange, unpractised giggling.

∞   ∞   ∞

Kristal wandered around her apartment vacantly, trying to think of something to do with this very shitty day.

Kristal went into her kitchen and grabbed the huge bird-whistle. "I'll take one more crack at her," she muttered, putting it into her mouth and crossing over to the window. She found that she couldn't even open it, so strong was the wind outside. "Big storm coming," Kristal said, staring at the thick black sky.

Kristal decided that the thing to do would be to read a book. Logan had leant her a book a month or so back, come to think, and there it was on the bookshelf right where she'd left it, and Kristal picked it up and discovered it was called *The Dogstar*, written by a fellow named Professor Percy St.J. Quodmon, and Kristal thought, what in the world? She flipped it open and read:

On September 23, Bernard Humbolt was taking his morning coffee on his back veranda. As he sipped his drink, he watched as a space conveyance from beyond our Solar System landed in his back garden, ruining the rhododen-drons. From this six-foot circular vehicle emerged two beings: a short, green man and a tall, hovering, silver woman. These beings approached Humbolt and handed him a *plate of pancakes*. This was to be the first of many encounters with the inhabitants of the Dogstar Sirius.

"Get real," said Kristal, throwing the book back on the shelf. She'd read all her other books. She looked them over to see if one jumped up and demanded to be reread, but none did. Kristal went over to her apartment-sized piano and parked herself on the bench. She hit one of her weird chords. That made her feel better. She hit another, choice and brutal. *"I got nothing to do . . .,"* she improvised lyrics, *"except thinking of you . . ."* There was something wonky about the syntax, but Kristal didn't mind, there was something wonky about everything. *"The world is wonky,"* she began again, knowing she was writing herself into a corner. *"I'm in a honky . . . tonk."* This simple statement contained revelation; Kristal stood upright and snapped her fingers. "I got it!" she announced. "I'm going to go get *stinko.*"

∞   ∞   ∞

Don and Dan, respectively the colour man and the play-by-play commentator for "Hockey Night in Canada," had flown from Toronto to Ottawa earlier that morning. In Ottawa they hired a limousine to drive them to Falconbridge. Why they did this is best known to the bureaucracy of the Canadian Broadcasting Corporation. Falconbridge was admittedly a few miles closer to the nation's capital, and this was probably what prompted the course of action. It may have been a tactical error, because the small airplane from Toronto was whipped about by the ever-more menacing winds. Don and Dan, never comfortable in the air, demanded sizable amounts of alcohol. By the time the rented limo arrived in Falconbridge, the two were visibly hammered.

Don was the younger man, handsome only because there was nothing irregular about his appearance. Dan was some years older; his face looked like a road map. Every time Dan had yelled "HE SHOOTS! HE SCORES!" three or four veins had exploded. Dan's nose looked like a scarlet mushroom cloud. Dan's eyes were soft and unfocussed, mostly because they needed extremely thick bifocals, something Dan would only deign to in the privacy of his broadcasting booth.

Don and Dan marched into the office of Elmore Daisy, owner and general manager of the Falconbridge Falcons. Daisy was a small man, conservative and sombre in his dress. Don and Dan searched drunkenly for chairs and threw themselves down.

"Hello, Mr. Daisy!" said Don cheerfully.

Elmore smiled.

"Let's cut the crapola," snarled Dan. He was insulted that he hadn't been offered a drink.

"Would you gentlemen care for a drink?"

Don and Dan accepted, but Dan's mood was still black. "Let's cut the crapola," he began again. "Here's the pickle. Let us say we set up the cameras. Let us say we start filming the hockey game. Let us say it goes out LIVE TO ALL THE HOMES ACROSS CANADA AND IN NEWFOUNDLAND! All the nice families clustered around the television sets. Father, mother, brother, sister and infant. Father smoking pipe! Mother nursing infant! Brother pretending to be Rocket Richard! Sister playing with doll! The television is on. 'HOCKEY NIGHT IN CANADA.' Happiness! Contentment! The nuclear family, strong in the hinterland! The game begins. What-ho? HE SHOOTS! HE SCORES! Game over! Contentment vanished! Nuclear family disintegrating. Brother and sister turn to sex and drugs! Mother and father undergo painful divorce! Tragedy across our great nation!"

Tears began to roll over Dan's wrinkled face. Elmore Daisy quickly poured him another drink.

"What Dan means," said Don, who was always saying *what Dan means*, "is this. Because of the very nature of the game, what with it being a sudden-death overtime, it could be over in ten seconds."

"Discontentment! Sorrow! Unhappiness!" said Dan.

"It's a possibility," admitted Elmore Daisy. "On the other

hand, they've played fifteen periods without a goal being scored. That is, after all, why you've come."

Don pulled his chair toward Elmore's desk. "Mr. Daisy, we were looking for a little . . . insurance."

"Yes?"

"What we'd like," spoke Don quietly, "is one sure period. You see what I'm getting at? We'd like to be sure of getting at least one period of hockey."

"I'm sure you will," said Elmore Daisy.

"We'd like a guarantee," said Don, almost in a whisper.

"What is it you wish me to do? Go to the players and say, nobody score a goal for at least a period?"

Don and Dan both nodded.

Elmore Daisy rose slowly from behind his desk. "Would you gentlemen wait here for just a minute, please?" Daisy slipped out of his office.

Don turned to Dan. "You don't say Newfoundland anymore, Dan. They became part of Canada in 1948."

"ALL THE HOMES ACROSS CANADA AND IN NEWFOUNDLAND!" chirped Dan automatically.

"No." Don spoke sternly. "All the homes across Canada."

"ALL THE HOMES ACROSS CANADA," repeated Dan. "ALL THE HOMES ACROSS CANADA."

In the middle of his fifth repetition the office door flew open and in stepped a man wearing an ornate rhinestone cowboy suit. On his head there was a Stetson and in his hand there was a bullwhip. He made this weapon crack savagely near the two broadcasters.

"You two are lower than snake bellies!" cried Buck Tanager. "You're lucky I don't run you out of town with them mic'aphone dingies shoved up your rosy-roos!"

"Madness! Insanity! A surreal aspect to the proceedings!" screamed Dan.

Buck Tanager lashed out with the bullwhip. He'd never wielded the thing before, but he seemed to have a knack. Buck neatly flicked Don's toupee from the man's crown. It was a

convincing enough display to send Don racing out of the office;
Dan followed quickly on his partner's heels.

"I'll guarantee you shit!" Buck Tanager yelled after them.
For effect, Buck lashed out with his whip one final time. He
wrapped the end around a Tiffany lamp and deftly lobbed it
through the window. Then Buck went to change back into his
Elmore Daisy clothes before he did any more damage.

∞   ∞   ∞

For the kind of stinko Kristal Donahue had in mind, the kind of
stinko that was soul-searching and pan-galactic at the same
time (the kind that Logan specialized in), there was really only
one place to go: the Dove Hotel.

The Dove was quite a nice-looking establishment from the
outside. It reminded Kristal of some Southern colonial
mansion, a bright white building with a big veranda and
scrolled pillars. A sign swung above the front door, a fading
piece of wood painted with some alien's impression of a dove.
The wind was causing the sign to swing madly, the rusting
chains howled. Bravely, she pushed open the door.

Kristal had expected the Dove to be wall-to-wall with
gnarled and shrivelled people, but the place was quiet
and empty. One man (admittedly far advanced in a gnarled
and shrivelled way) sat in a corner, smoking cigarettes and
seemingly not drinking his quart bottle of beer. June the
barmaid was leaning against the jukebox and watching a soap
opera on the overhead television screen. June liked soap
operas; the tiny worlds evolved in a way she could understand,
their God was a dull person. The bartender was reading a
newspaper behind the bar, and occasionally conversing with a
man sitting on the stool opposite, a man who Kristal recognized
thankfully as Joe Fineweather.

Kristal climbed up on the stool beside his. The bartender, a
stout older man, allowed his eyebrows to scoot up on his
forehead. He hadn't seen too many ladies of Kristal's sort even

enter the Dove, let alone willingly climb up on a barstool beside Joe Fineweather.

Our friend Joseph took it in stride. He turned, grinned his wandering grin, and said, "Greetings, Kristal."

Kristal was surprised that Joe knew her name, although with all due modesty she was by way of being a celebrity, at least in Falconbridge, for playing piano at Birds of a Feather and seeing Logan.

Kristal, making conversation, remarked, "Big storm coming."

"You're telling me!" Joe made a little "sheesh" and whapped himself on the forehead.

Kristal ordered a drink—the draught beer looked reasonably safe—and said, "So, Joe, how about them Falcons?"

"How about them?" responded Joe, friendly enough but to no real point.

"Who's gonna win that game?"

Joe shrugged. "Whoever scores first," he assessed accurately. "Mind you, Logan can't lose."

"I see." They sat in silence for a few moments. "Well, Mr. Fineweather," said Kristal Donahue finally, "I tried weather and I tried sports. I thought that's what people talked about in barrooms."

Joe Fineweather laughed, reminding Kristal of a trout jumping in a lakeful of ale. "Me," judged Joe Fineweather, "I'm into more general things. Sports and weather are too specific. I mean, what can you do about the weather?"

Kristal shrugged, pursed her lips and said, "Sweet dee-ay."

"Wrong! You can fight tooth and nail! But there's no sense in sitting around and talking about it. Now, sports I don't really understand. Team sports, what a concept. Have you been to the hockey arena?"

"Yeah."

"Very *mysterioso*," whispered Joe. "White people magic. I wouldn't touch it with a stick."

"I didn't notice much magic going on," said Kristal.

Joe shrugged. "Is that why you've decided to get stinko?"

"How'd you know that?"

"Easy," said Joe. "A look in your eyes. A feeling. Not to mention, you downed that beer in about a minute flat."

Kristal ordered another. "So, let's talk general."

"It's all very strange," remarked Joe Fineweather in a general way.

"Let's talk specifics," Kristal suggested.

"Logan's very strange."

"Now we're getting somewhere."

More booze was purchased.

Fifteen

In the early afternoon the strangely dressed little lad came back into Li's Hardware. Logan was standing behind the counter reading the Sports section of the Toronto *Star* (which had also printed the already semifamous photograph). The boy levelled his gaze at Logan.

Logan looked up slowly. "Yo?"

"Salutations, Mr. Logan. I was wondering if you would kindly chase me out of the establishment?"

Logan shrugged. The ancient Chinese midget Li was currently out on business and Logan was bored and a little lonely.

Little Anthony's eyes lighted on the sports page. His day had gone so strangely—he'd spread out his notebooks, made a major breakthrough regarding his topology theorem, and then suddenly Anthony had marched outside without so much as a thought—that he'd neglected to check the scores, a chore he invariably did while eating his tomato sandwich at lunch. "Would you mind giving me last evening's results?"

Logan's eyes romped about the page. "Let me see here. Toronto beat Washington," he said, "four to two. Montreal beat Detroit, seven to four. Edmonton beat Calgary, six to five. That's all she wrote."

Little Anthony nodded abstractly, revising his mentally stored statistics.

"Who's your favourite team?" asked Logan.

The question bewildered Anthony, causing him to blink his eyes rapidly. "Montreal," was the only thing he could think to say, "is currently in the forefront of the league standings."

"Sure, but who do you like?"

"Many of the teams are very good. Some of the recent franchises exist in a state of proemial nonage, but want only time's passing before they too achieve respectability." Anthony went to adjust his spectacles instinctively, which he would have done except that he had twenty-twenty vision and didn't wear them.

"Who's your favourite player?"

Again, an odd thing to ask. "I suggest to you that Mr. Guy LaPlante currently leads all scoring categories. Last night's game excluded for want of information, he has amassed thus far thirty-seven goals and forty-nine assists."

"He got the hat-trick last night."

Anthony programmed that information.

"So he's your favourite?" persisted Logan.

"I see no reason to make such a declaration."

Logan stared at the little kid for a long moment. "You're sort of peculiar, aren't you?"

"When you were my age, did you have a favourite player?"

"For sure."

"Very well, then, I must have one. How should I proceed?"

"Proceed?"

"I refer to the process of favourite player selection."

"Oh, yeah." Logan rubbed his hands together, getting excited somewhere deep in his being. "Do like this. Close your eyes and start to think. Okay. Maybe Guy LaPlante is your favourite, and you just don't know about it yet. So we're gonna think about Guy. And I can see something. Can you see it, But?"

"I see nothing, as my eyes are closed per your instructions."

"I can see the St. Lawrence River. It's all frozen up because, hell, is it cold. And little Guy is out on the ice, all alone. He's got about fourteen sweaters on, that's how goddamn cold it is. It hurts to breathe out there. Guy's nostrils are stuck together and his lips are blue as the sky. But Guy's been out there practising, skating around on the river and waiting for the big guys to come. And when they come, they tell him to take a scamper. And Guy says, hey, let me play, and they say, give us a dollar, and it's all the money little Guy's ever had in his life, but he gives it to them and they let him play. And little Guy starts dancing. He's not skating, he's goddamn dancing out there on the big frozen river. And little Guy gets the puck and waltzes through everybody. He's calling the shots, all the shots, just dancing and dipsydoodling, and he puts the puck into the net and no one could have stopped him."

"I dare say perhaps yourself or Bram Ridout might have!"

Logan laughed. "I don't know if I'd want to."

Anthony tried to visualize Guy LaPlante in this manner. He stared at the darkness inside of himself. Something began to appear, something wide and white. A frozen river. For an instant, Anthony thought he could see a little boy out on the ice.

"Try one on your own," suggested Logan.

"Very well. I shall attempt to visualize internally Mr. Lanny McDermott," Anthony said, choosing the player at random. He shut his eyes. First of all McDermott's statistics came goose-stepping across his mind; Anthony brushed them away. He concentrated as hard as he could. After a moment he opened his eyes, defeated and sad. "Nothing. I saw nothing."

"That's right," Logan nodded.

"It is?"

"McDermott is a prairie boy. You were looking at the goddamn prairie in the middle of the winter. What did you expect to see?"

Happily, Anthony buttoned up his eyes. Yes, it is the prairie, a lonely place. It's hard to make out anything, but right in the middle of all the nothingness there appears to be a . . . a . . .

"A skating rink."

"You bet," nodded Logan.

Anthony moved, in his mind and in the hardware store, a little closer to the boards. He saw a little boy with red hair putting on his skates. The boy was doing something peculiar. He was stuffing newspapers down the sides of his skates. Anthony informed Mr. Logan of this aberrant behaviour.

"Yeppers," said Logan. "Because he's from a poor family, and he's just got old hand-me-down skates."

Little Lanny started practising his slapshot. Boom! It sounded loud as thunder as the shots came off the boards. The earth was empty except for that sound.

"Are you doing it?" whispered Logan.

"Yes." Anthony kept his eyes shut until Logan nudged him gently. "I was doing it!" Master O'Toole cried happily. "I was indulging in the internalized visualization of a famous hockey player's formative years!"

"Or, you could call that there *daydreaming*."

"I've heard of it," acknowledged Anthony. "Perhaps I shall forthwith daydream Bobby Orr." Anthony screwed his eyes shut and smiled.

∞   ∞   ∞

It was two hours later that Anthony O'Toole finally left Li's Hardware. The lad kept his eyes screwed shut and bounced, unbothered, off walls and doorframes. Luk Sun Li, the ancient Chinese dwarf, was back in the store reorganizing the shelves. Li did this whenever there were no customers, which meant that the stock was in a constant state of flux.

The telephone rang. Luk Sun Li floated over and plucked up the receiver gingerly. Li was somehow afraid of the telephone, mostly because it seemed to him that everyone on the other end screamed. Li held the receiver about a foot away from his ear and said a polite "Hurro?"

Luk Sun Li listened to the voice at the other end and nodded. He was forever nodding and bowing to people on the phone. "Famous Mr. Logan!" Li sang out. "Someone wishes to speak with the famous, illustrious Logan!"

"Who is it?" Logan asked suspiciously.

"As to that, I do not know. It is a lady," was the best Li could do.

Logan's heart wanted to answer the phone, on the off-chance it was Kristal. Logan's mind wasn't so sure, but it played along with the heart out of pity. Logan took the receiver. "Yeah?"

When he heard the voice, Logan looked down at his dick and whispered, "It's for you." His little buddy the hard-on tried to jump all the way to the telephone but was thwarted by Logan's belt.

It was Darla Featherstone, the perfect social calendar/weather woman.

Logan listened, distracted, as Darla said some things he didn't understand. Television words kept cropping up, *format*, *one on one dialogue*, weird stuff like that. The phrase "A Woman's Diary" was repeated often. "Can you do it?" Darla asked finally.

"I sure can."

"Five o'clock then."

"Five," repeated Logan. He replaced the receiver and stared straight ahead for a long moment.

Luk Sun Li prodded Logan with a long nail he happened to be holding. "So, prestigious and notable Logan, who was that on the telephone?"

"Darla."

"DARLA!" Li's face did something disgusting. Logan found it crude and off-putting.

"She wants me to be on TV," said Logan.

"Logan has achieved pre-eminence!" Luk Sun Li giggled furiously. "Which programme are you to be on?"

Logan mumbled, "A Woman's Diary."

Li stabbed one of his invisible fingers toward Logan and hooted. "Logan is not a woman!" he pointed out. And then he became serious. "And 'A Woman's Diary' is on at five-thirty."

"Yeah?"

Luk Sun Li floated closer to Logan. "The show is on at five-thirty, and yet my establishment remains open until six. What happens if the tourist trade arrives?" Li crossed his tiny arms and fumed.

"There is no effing tourist trade!" protested Logan. "Who the hell would come to Falconbridge?"

"Maybe people to see the renowned Mr. Logan!" screamed Luk Sun Li sarcastically. The madder Li got, the worse his English became. By this time he was addressing his adversary as *Rohgun*. "If no tourist trade, why the hell I got you?"

"Why?" responded Rohgun. "You got me so you can walk around pretending you're some Zen fucking philosopher, that's why. *Playing out of peacefulness*. Horse apples."

"Rohgun," snapped Luk Sun Li, "take a hike."

Logan nodded and grabbed his coat.

"And another thing, Rohgun. Goo' ruck."

"Goo' ruck?"

"Tonight at hockey. Goo' ruck."

"Right. Thanks."

As soon as he stepped outside Logan was pushed down the street by a huge gust of wind. Logan fell down heavily and bruised his hip. He raised himself back to his feet with the aid of a lamp standard. Logan bundled his coat and picked his way carefully toward the television station. Halfway there he ducked into Hubie's Open Kitchen for a cup of coffee.

Hubie had the Sports section from the *Star* spread out all over the counter. The picture of Logan was featured in the middle of the page.

"You see this?" asked Hubie.

"It's just in because it's a good photo," said Logan modestly.

"Not that. This about Lindy Olver."

Logan hadn't seen anything about Lindy. He'd looked at the Sports section all day, but mostly he'd gazed at his own grainy image. Logan grabbed the paper from Hubie and started to read.

Lindy Olver and Logan had played on the same team twice, the second time in Atlanta. At that time, Lindy was at the peak of his career. Lindy was, according to almost everyone, probably the most naturally gifted athlete to ever play hockey. Sportswriters couldn't get their prose purple enough to describe his skill. But, as even his most ardent supporters had to admit, Olver had certain personality problems. For a long while he'd gotten into drugs and alcohol (especially when on the same team as Logan) and the low point of his career came one sad night when Lindy received a fairly hard bodycheck and threw up voluminously on coast-to-coast television. The next day the newspapers reported that Lindy Olver was through. But the next day, the papers took it all back. Lindy Olver had found the Lord.

Olver's reappearance was dazzling. The very next year he led his team to the Stanley Cup. Over the summer Olver published his autobiography, *Jesus Is My Linemate*, in which he criticized everyone on his team with the exception of an assistant trainer (himself a Born Again Christian) and, of course, his linemate Jesus. Lindy criticized everyone in professional hockey and, eventually, everyone in professional sport. When he reported for training camp he was traded. Reports leaked out that he wasn't fitting in with his new team, that he sermonized in the lockerroom and demanded that his teammates seek salvation above all else. Meanwhile, of course, Olver played beautifully, without anyone's assistance or encouragement. He was traded soon enough, and this cycle was repeated over and over for a couple of years.

The article, pointed out by Hubie, confirmed what Jay had told Logan the day before, that Lindy had cleared waivers. No team was willing to put up with his proselytizing ways, despite

the magnificence of his abilities. Lindy, with his boundless
Born Again spirit, had risen above it all. He was quoted:

> I love the Lord my Saviour and I love the game of hockey.
> Hockey is the most important thing in my life, next to the
> Lord and His Infinite Love. So I will continue to play hockey.
> I understand that my home town team would be more than
> willing to have me back.

Logan skipped to the last line of the article, just in case his
memory was playing tricks with him. It wasn't.

Lindy Olver is a native of Hope, Ontario.

Sixteen

Kristal Donahue, some beers later, motioned at the bartender. "Excuse me," she said, "but we need two Birdbaths. Immediately. Do you know how to make a Birdbath?"

The bartender shook his head sheepishly. He wasn't entirely sure how to make a scotch and soda.

"My confrere Mr. Fineweather will inform you," said Kristal.

"A Birdbath," Mr. Fineweather tried to remember. He waved his hand at the liquor bottles vaguely.

"Exactly," nodded Kristal enthusiastically. "And there'll be a big tip in it for you if you can get us to the airport in fifteen minutes."

The bartender shrugged and fetched two beer mugs. He improvised freely, grabbing bottles and pouring either small dollops or stiff belts.

"Well," said Kristal, receiving her drink, "here's to your health!"

They raised their glasses and tapped them together.

"Hey, Joey," Kristal said, spreading her arms across the bar for added support, "do you know what happened to Logan's legs?"

"One night," nodded Joe Fineweather, "Logan and I were drinking together. And I asked him. He said something about mindfuckers from the Dogstar Sirius."

144

"Oh," said Kristal, "you must mean the Serious Dog-star."

"Whatever," Joe shrugged. "Anyway, a little later we were drunker, so I asked him again. And he said something about his buddy Lindy."

"Lindy Olver? What about him?"

"Ask Lindy, that's what Logan said." Joe Fineweather gestured at his glass irritably. "Worst Birdbath I ever had."

Kristal drained her mug in a few long pulls. "Tell you what. Let's go get a Birds of a Feather Birdbath. If that don't get us stinko, nothing will."

"Okee-dokee." Joe more or less fell off his barstool, and Kristal's dismount was hardly lady-like.

The bar had filled up in the time she'd spent drinking with Joe. There were at least seven people now, all men, and fully six of them could be described as *withered*. Somehow this failed to depress Kristal beyond words. Instead she grinned at them in turn and said, "G'day, lads."

They nodded uncertainly.

"We're off," she informed them. "This is a nice place, but they serve a lousy Birdbath."

Kristal put her arm around Joe Fineweather's shoulder and they left the Dove Hotel.

∞   ∞   ∞

"Now this sucker here," announced Kristal, holding the vessel up to her eyes and staring through at a strange world, "this here is what you call your Birdbath." She took a sip and belched; the belch inspired Joe Fineweather to speech.

"Once, when I was a child . . ."

Kristal immediately set down her drink and cradled her head in her hands. She imagined that she was four years old and sitting on her great-grandfather's knee. Her great-grandfather, Louis Proulx, fisherman and Micmac, had drowned in the ocean years before Kristal had been born.

"I was sitting all alone in our house. Our house was never in the best shape, and there were holes in the roof." Joe pointed at imaginary holes. "So as I was sitting there, guess what?"

"What?"

"A squirrel fell through the roof and landed on me. And the squirrel was frightened, so he bit me. Lookee." Joe held out one of his hands for inspection. "Scars. And the thing about it is, for a long time—years even—I was afraid of squirrels. I thought that squirrels were nasty vicious little pricks who would attack for no reason. I'm still a little afraid of squirrels, which is embarrassing for such an outdoorsy type. But you see my point, right?"

Kristal looked for it desperately. "Wrong."

"I think it happens to a lot of people with love. Love falls through a hole in the roof, gets frightened and bites them. And after that, they're afraid of love."

Kristal turned her head away, meaning to chaw this poser through in a philosophical manner. She was confronted by Koko. The bird stared at her with an awful arrogance.

"Oh, yeah?" snapped Kristal. "What would *you* know about it?"

Koko dealt out a sneering caw and waddled farther down the bar. Koko was allowed out of her cage when there weren't many customers in Birds of a Feather, and there certainly weren't. There were, in fact, three. The third was a short square woman with a brushcut. She stood at the bar some feet down from Joseph and Kristal. This woman's mission in life seemed to be the smoking of cigarettes.

Koko paused in front of Joe Fineweather; the two stared at each other for a long moment. Finally Koko dismissed Joe with a feathered shrug and wandered away.

Kristal drummed her fingernails against the empty vessel. "Keep them Birdbaths coming," she called.

∞   ∞   ∞

The local CBC affiliate was housed in a tiny building, two stories high and perfectly square. Logan had been inside it once before (he couldn't recall why, probably an attempted assassination of either King McGeek or Buck Tanager/Elmore Daisy) and knew that usually the lobby's sole occupant was a very slender old lady who designated herself MRS. BOYD BOYCE via a nameplate on her desk. Logan was acquainted with Boyd Boyce and wondered why Mrs. Boyd was so proud of the fact that she was married to him.

On that day, however, the small station was wall-to-wall people. They were by and large technicians, burly fellows with Caterpillar caps, down-filled vests and enormous potbellies. Mrs. Boyd Boyce looked distinctly green. Her desk and immediate surroundings insistently displayed signs that read THANK YOU FOR NOT SMOKING. The cameramen and audio guys didn't seek her gratitude.

Mrs. Boyd waved through a heavy grey cloud. "Yoohoo! Mr. Logan!"

Things are certainly strange when people are glad to see me, mused Logan. He felt dissatisfied.

"I'm on 'A Woman's Diary,' " he said upon reaching the desk of Mrs. Boyd Boyce.

"Oh, yes, yes, I know you are, Mr. Logan. Ms. Featherstone's special topic this week is an in-depth up-close look at the world of men, you know, and you're just the fellow she wants to talk to."

"Yeah?"

"And I'd just like to say how proud everyone in the town is of you."

Logan was stunned. "Everyone in the town is proud of me?"

"Yeppers, sonny-jim. We think you're the bee's knees."

"Shit . . .," muttered Logan unhappily.

∞　　　∞　　　∞

"Mickey Moonie, that's me," said the little woman, shaking hands with Joe and Kristal in a no-nonsense kind of way. "Ace reporter."

"I'm Kristal Donahue. Lounge pianist. This is my personal friend and business associate Joseph Fineweather."

"Professional mystic. Amateur weatherman," added Uncle Joe.

"Me," announced Mickey Moonie, "I'm all ears."

This was alarming news to Joe Fineweather. Even with his weak eyes he could see that this woman was less ears than anybody else in the world. She had two tiny folds of skin about the size of postage stamps affixed to her head where her brushcut ended.

"I've been listening," explained the woman. She whipped out a reporter's notepad and flipped it open. "Here it is. *Logan,* says the chickie. *What about him?* asks the geezer. *Still wondering about those knees,* she says." Mickey Moonie snapped the notepad shut. "It's my job," she offered a bit apologetically. "Now, I'm here to cover the game. Trouble is, so is every ragdog in the province. So I start thinking angle. I start thinking human interest. Then I remember, Logan's a gimp. I start investigating. I get on the blower, make a few calls. Talk to the police and a hospital down in Atlanta. So I got the lowdown. Ask away."

"What happened to Logan's legs?" Kristal obeyed.

"They got fuggin' crunched! The doctors told me that Logan doesn't really have anything you could call knees. He's got some fancy metal junk and a bunch of air, and that's about it. Jeez, when I told the sawbones that Logan was still a shinnyman, he just about crapped petunias. He said he hadn't figured on Logan ever walking right again."

"But what *happened* to them?"

"I'm still working on it," admitted Mickey Moonie. "Here's what I got so far. Happened in Atlanta. Happened in the parking lot of a place called Kenny's Road House. Logan was walking in the parking lot. Logan was pissed as a newt. He got hit by a car driven by a Nester Spiggot. I got Spiggot's number, but I haven't been able to reach him."

"I know what he'll say," said Kristal. "I'll just bet the old farthead Logan was wandering around with his face stuck up in the air, trying to find those damn constellations."

"I'll bet Logan was singing that song and crying so he couldn't see the car," offered Joe Fineweather.

"Why don't I try Nester again?" Mickey Moonie fished around in her pocket and took out several empty cigarette packages, all of which had phone numbers and/or little messages scrawled on them. She sorted through until she found one—SPIGGOT, it said, in crippled block letters—and raced off to the payphone.

Kristal happened to look up at the bar television and saw that there was a show on. "A Woman's Diary" rolled by in a flowery script over the set, which consisted of two long sofas and a coffee table.

On one sofa sat the bimbo Darla Featherstone. She was devastatingly beautiful, a joke on God's part. Darla held a clipboard and consulted it occasionally.

Kristal wasn't surprised to see Logan sitting on the other couch. Kristal wouldn't have been surprised to see Logan playing hopscotch with the Queen Mother. She was a little alarmed at how ugly the goof was, a long gash in his cheek, a black eye, a split lip.

Logan seemed uncomfortable on the sofa. He shifted his weight around, trying to settle in, but the cushions kept sinking beneath him. Logan was also continually tempted to rest the heels of his filthy salt-stained cowboy boots on the coffee table, but some vestigial recollection of good manners prevented him.

From farther along the bar came a sudden and horrendous howl. Koko stood transfixed by the sight of his favourite human being on the television. The cockatoo stared at Logan, tilted his head in disbelief and then let loose another scream. Joseph squinted and strained and pulled at his old eyes, and then smiled. "Lookee," he said, "Logan."

The bartender came and cranked up the volume.

"—viously a very violent game," said Darla.

Logan opened his mouth to say something but never did. He decided to nod instead. He nodded for a good long time.

"We need go no further than your own face for proof," pointed out Darla.

"I got the shi—" Logan started. Then he nodded a few more times.

Mickey Moonie came bustling back from the phone in the corner. She saw that Logan was on the TV, so she launched herself onto a barstool to watch. First she whipped out a lighter and produced a giant lick of flame, almost a foot long. She got her cigarette going and had it down to the filter in five puffs.

Kristal nudged her in the side. "What did you find out?"

"Sssh. I'll tell you after the programme."

Koko let out one more unearthly howl, still waiting for Logan to respond.

Darla asked Logan, "When you make a save, do you think the feeling could accurately be described as orgasmic?"

Logan looked perplexed. He seemed to answer in a code transmitted via eye-blinks.

"I'm not asking if you actually ejaculate, but are there similarities?"

Mickey took out a new cigarette. "Who's the bimbo?"

"Darla Featherstone," Kristal answered, taking pains to make the name sound ridiculous.

"Mr. Logan seems a touch embarrassed by this line of questioning," Darla told the camera. "He is obviously not comfortable with his sexuality."

Logan shrugged, this statement having the ring of authenticity.

Darla picked up another line of questioning. "Mr. Logan, why do you play goal?"

"Well, I'm kind of good at it."

"It is compensatory?"

"It's what?"

"I suggest there are some areas in your life in which you're not good," Darla explained eagerly. "Sexual areas."

"Lady—"

"Darla."

"How come all you want to talk about is sex?"

"Am I making you nervous?"

Kristal wasn't watching; she had little interest in the man on the television screen. Koko had turned away, deeply hurt and confused.

"I think it's manifestly clear," said Darla, "that sports are an outlet for sexual frustration."

Logan crossed his arms and looked at Darla for a long while. "Can we talk about something else now?"

"Shall we discuss penis size?"

"Let's not."

"Aha!"

Logan leaned forward. "I have something to discuss which is very, very important. Something I feel the whole world should know about before it's too late."

"And what might that be?"

Logan answered simply and succinctly. "Mindfuckers from the Dogstar Sirius."

The show came out live, so there was little anybody could do about the language. Darla told Logan, sternly, to keep it clean.

"But that's what they're called!" Logan protested innocently.

"I'm trying to have a serious conversation."

"I'm trying to have a Sirius conversation. Haven't you noticed how complicated everything has become? There has obviously been outside interference, and all the evidence points toward the Dogstar Sirius." Logan crossed his arms with finality.

"Mr. Logan, I can't tell if you're being serious."

"That's one of their weapons! Don't you see? The mindfuckers come down and make everything too serious." Logan slapped the couch suddenly. "You want to know how bad it's getting? There's a little girl named Charlene, and I've never seen her laugh or play with a doll. And there's this little boy who dresses funny, and he doesn't even know how to dream. And Kristal doesn't laugh anymore. And how about the kid, eh? Bram. Talk about serious, that kid's about to explode."

"Mr. Logan, you seem a little distraught."

Logan threw himself back into the sofa. "You never been there."

Koko let out a regal response to Logan's speech. He puffed himself up as if appointing himself Official Protector against the imminent invasion of Sirius mindfuckers.

Darla Featherstone gazed at Logan with obvious affection. "We'll have more of this later," Darla said mysteriously. "Now I have to do the social calendar."

"Enough of this garbage," snapped Kristal, stinko on Birdbaths. "What's the story on Logan's legs?"

Mickey Moonie lit a butt, ordered a drink and said, "You know this guy Lindy Olver?"

∞   ∞   ∞

Lindy Olver was racing toward Falconbridge in his silver BMW. The weather was rapidly turning foul—high winds, nasty flurries—but Lindy was driving as if he was in Monaco. He kept the gas pedal pressed firmly to the floor and passed other vehicles without notice of corners or hills. A couple of times the car hit an icy patch and started to fishtail, but Lindy never considered slowing down. He was in no real hurry to get to Falconbridge, he was just usually in a hurry.

Lindy Olver plugged in a cassette of Ernest Angley, the famous faith-healing evangelist. Lindy had once travelled all the way to Akron, Ohio, to hear Angley preach. It had been the most thrilling moment of his Born Again life, and when Ernest Angley had called the people forward to be healed, Lindy joined the queue ecstatically. Then Lindy remembered that there was nothing wrong with him. In fact, he was damned near perfect. With a heavy heart, Lindy had to sit back down.

Lindy caught himself grinning. Thinking about Ernest Angley had reminded a remote part of Lindy's brain about something Logan had once done. Lindy Olver shook his head clear of such memories before acknowledging that he'd had them. He listened to Angley's voice and tried to convince himself that he'd found inner peace.

∞   ∞   ∞

Now Logan was a professional athlete who didn't often act like one. The same can't be said of his hard-on. As soon as the little fellow caught drift of the rumour that he might be called upon, he began strenuous pregame warm-ups – jumping jacks and windsprints on the sidelines.

Darla took Logan upstairs to her dressingroom. Wordlessly, she began to disrobe. Logan's mind was too weary to deal with it. He watched her get naked. It wasn't the body that Logan had dreamt. Darla's navel was of the sort that protrudes and she had a short crescent-shaped scar on her right thigh. Logan thought about his beautiful Fiberglas goaler's mask, the one that transformed his face into a mighty soaring eagle.

Darla climbed aboard a sofa, agonizingly naked. Darla ordered Logan to do several things. Logan did them as best he could. Darla refused to let Logan touch her left breast, claiming it was too sensitive; she demanded that all his attention be focussed on the right. She complained of too much friction on her protruding belly-button and private places. As they got going, she barked out orders like a marine drill sergeant. She told Logan that he was going too fast, a moment later she told him for god's sake speed things up. Darla suggested pointedly that he attempt a bizarrely geometric motion not unlike a

Möbius strip. Logan did as well as he could with a mind full of *Weltschmerz*, Harriet Rollins, little Charlene Luttor.

Darla seemed to be attending a Dancercize class. The only one having any fun was Logan's hard-on.

Darla suddenly became loud, gasping, moaning, calling out to God.

Logan thought of other things.

"Mindfuckers!" Darla screamed.

The world was lost a moment later.

Seventeen

D on and Dan, still shaken after the attack by a rhinestone-studded, bullwhip-cracking desperado, had gone off in search of alcohol. They had stumbled into a place called the Dove, where they were recognized immediately by the patrons, a dozen gnarled and withered specimens. "Don and Dan!" the Dove inhabitants roared. Don and Dan smiled politely, muttered thank-yous. "Fuck you guys!" the Dovites returned. So Don and Dan had stumbled down the length of King Street, fighting against the wind, until they arrived at a place called Birds of a Feather.

Inside, Birds of a Feather looked like a tropical rain forest. Plants and vines and ferns covered the walls and ceiling, they curled around pillars and table legs. Don and Dan, Canadian lads both, broke into heavy sweats and tore off their sheepskin coats. "Torrid. Sweltering. Steamy," mumbled Dan. Don looked around and saw that most of the action was at the long bar. He grabbed Dan by the shirtsleeve and dragged him over.

It was, several signs announced, Happy Hour. That made Don happy. The signs told him he could get two Birdbaths for the price of one. Don ordered these Birdbaths and Dan (who had just coined the term *perspirational*) thought he'd died and gone to Heaven. "Enormous. Mountainous. Colossal." Don and Dan set to work on these concoctions with great energy.

"Don and Dan?" came a strange voice, and they turned, to be confronted by a square brushcutted little woman, who reached out a tiny hand and said, "Mickey Moonie, *Daily Planet*. Nice to see you. Can I buy you a drink or what?"

Meanwhile, Kristal was about to start work. She'd wrestled into one of her sequined lounge pianist dresses. That struggle left her sweating and exhausted. The bar was quiet that night; the only person huddled over drinks at her piano was Joseph Fineweather.

Kristal parked her behind on the piano bench and her manic hands violated the keyboard. Joe F. reared back in alarm.

"Any requests?" demanded Kristal.

"Stop," requested Joe.

"I got a scoop," announced Mickey Moonie. (Don and Dan were now the proud owners of no less than four Birdbaths apiece, although Dan, with his weak unbifocaled eyes, imagined that he owned many more.) "And I'll let you have it, if you say my name on TV and say how it was my investigative reporting that came up with it."

"Scoop," repeated Don.

"Ladle. Dipper. Spoon," said Dan.

"It's about Logan."

Don wanted stuff about Logan. The "Hockey Night in Canada" research staff had been decidedly substandard in that regard. Indeed, all they'd come up with was Logan's first initial, the numbers from his short stay in the NHL, and his place of birth.

Mickey Moonie flipped through her notepages until she hit the most recent, which was titled SCOOP. "Scene," she read, "the parking lot at Kenny's Road House. Two men walking along. One is Logan. One is Lindy Olver."

"Okay, okay, okay. I shall now play 'Try to 'Member,' but I don't want any friggin' crying. You got that, Fineweather? One teardrop on this baby grand, I'm out of here, kiss my butt bye-bye, hang my picture on your wall. Here we go."

It was a pretty simple scoop. Dan wasn't all that interested, being play-by-play, but to Don the colour man it was a little nugget of gold.

"The name's Moonie. Mickey Moonie. Try to remember."

"*When life was so tender* . . ." Kristal's voice quickly became thick and twisted. "Fuggit," she announced. "I'm goin' to the hockey game." She pulled her ski jacket over her strapless lounge pianist's gown and headed out into the black winter.

Joe Fineweather followed.

∞　　　∞　　　∞

Little Anthony O'Toole shoved away his dinner plate with the veal cutlet half eaten. "Well, Mater," he announced, "I'm presently off to attend the hockey game."

Mrs. O'Toole's veal cutlet was likewise half eaten. She was drinking a bloody Caesar and smoking a cigarette. She waved her hand disgustedly. "You have to stay in, it's a school-night."

"I do not attend school, ergo, the point is hardly germane."

"Can't you talk bloody English?" roared Mrs. O'Toole. She had, earlier that day, received an imaginative phone call from somewhere in Florida, her husband claiming that convoluted business dealings had delayed his return home. There had been giggling in the background.

"I reiterate my intention of attending the hockey game."

"You are going to eat your dinner, then you are going to bed."

"Mama," said little Anthony, "suck eggs."

Mrs. O'Toole drained her drink and placed the empty glass on the table. "WHAT THE HELL DID YOU SAY?"

"Quote, suck eggs, end of quote."

Mrs. O'Toole reached across the table and smacked Anthony sharply across the cheek. Anthony stared at her, his lip trembling, and then he started to cry. "I wanna go to the hockey game! I wanna go to the hockey game!" Anthony raised his tiny feet and began to beat his Oxfords against the underside of the table.

"All right!" shrieked Mrs. O'Toole. "All right, you bloody little twerp! Go to the hockey game!"

Anthony jumped from his chair and ran upstairs to get his things. When he got back down he saw his mother standing by the front door wearing her leopard-skin coat.

Little Anthony had stopped crying; his mother had started. "There's going to be a terrible storm," said Mrs. O'Toole. "I'd better go with you."

Tentatively, Anthony reached forward to take her hand.

∞   ∞   ∞

There was no such trouble at the Luttor household. Both Charlene and Lottie were anxious and eager to get to the game.

Carl Luttor was working harder than he ever had before, collecting bills while bathed in a crimson sweat. Carl Luttor got angry when he saw Joe Fineweather weaving his way toward the turnstile.

"Okay, Fineweather. Go away or I'll call the cops."

Joe grinned. "Carl, I got bad news for you." Joe peeled off his coat to reveal a FALCONBRIDGE FALCONS hockey jersey. Then he spun around like a fashion model so that Carl Luttor could see the back, where it said:

FINEWEATHER
ASS'T COACH

∞   ∞   ∞

A man smoking a pipe (sort of smoking; the thing was not lit) approached Carl Luttor and requested five tickets.

Carl Luttor, who didn't like people who smoked pipes, suspiciously eyed first this man, then the crew standing behind him. Nearly every member was quivering visibly. The exception was an old man dressed in a wizard's robes, who looked at the Falconbridge populace and announced, "Behold,

I will cause it to rain a very grievous hail, such as hath not been in Egypt since the foundation thereof even until now!" The old man flung imaginary lightning bolts with unbridled fury.

"Those people aren't from around here," noted Carl.

An old woman leapt out from the middle of the circle. She attacked the old man with the butt of an umbrella and the heel of a ballroom dancing shoe.

"Indeed not," said the bald man, who wore, under his heavy coat, the white dress of the medical profession.

"Are you ever asking for it!" shrieked the old man, covering his wizard's cap with liver-spotted hands. "It's murrain, boils and hail for you, Tootsie!"

"Where are you people from?" asked Carl Luttor craftily.

The old man was saved by a woman, six-foot-three and more than two hundred pounds. The woman looked like Logan in drag.

"We are just visiting," said the man, lighting a match and holding it over the cold bowl, "from South Grouse."

"Ha!" bellowed Carl. "What you got there, a bunch of loonies?"

A handsome young man broke from the circle and went down on one knee. "Swanee, how I love ya, how I love ya."

"Well," answered the man, producing little popping noises as he spoke, "I suppose you might say that."

"Hot damn!" shouted Carl. "They can't come in. There are decent people here. My granddaughter Charlene's in here." It was bad enough, Carl reflected, that he'd been forced to admit Joe Fineweather, damned if he was going to let in a bunch of crazy South Grousers.

"I am Dr. Louis Bermondsey. My son Warren plays on the team, you know."

"How about them over there? They're loons."

"These people," said Dr. Bermondsey, "are the Logans."

Carl handed over the tickets disgustedly. "Figures."

∞   ∞   ∞

Don and Dan were all made up and waiting for the commencement of "Hockey Night in Canada." They were also pie-eyed. They sat in Hockey Night in Canada chairs, in front of a backdrop covered with the Hockey Night in Canada logo.

The producer told them it was time to pretape an interview. For some reason Don chuckled mischievously. "Bring that sumbitch over here!"

Lindy Olver was brought in. Lindy had on his black jersey with HOPE spread across the chest. Lindy was remarkably handsome. With his golden hair and blue eyes, Lindy had become a huge star on the Christian Broadcasting Network. His appearances on "100 Huntley Street" and "The 700 Club" always produced large numbers of Born Again teen-aged girls and middle-aged women.

Lindy sat down between Don and Dan and played with a hockey stick, toying with an invisible puck.

Don conducted the interview. Dan was saving himself for the play-by-play and sleeping.

Don said, "Hello, Lindy."

Lindy smiled beatifically. "Hello, Donald."

Don hated being called Donald. He scowled and said, "It's pretty exciting in this town, wouldn't you say, Lindy?"

Lindy shrugged. Nothing the Lord could come up with was too wondrous for him.

Don shifted in his seat and assumed an interrogative side-saddle. "This is a bit of a reunion, isn't it, Lindy? For you and Logan, I mean."

Lindy nodded. "I know Logan. We were friends before I found the Lord. I've prayed many times for the redemption of Logan's soul."

"He seems like a nice enough guy to me."

Lindy looked downright sorrowful. "He is a drunkard and a fornicator."

Don laughed. "That's why I like him!"

The producer made various slashing motions at someone in the control booth, deleting Don's last statement.

"Satan has been very successful with Logan," proceeded Lindy. "And more's the pity, because Logan has a good heart."

"What makes you say that?" snapped Don.

Lindy looked momentarily confused. "Personal knowledge."

"Did he ever do anything for you?"

Lindy sidestepped neatly into his testimony. "I was once no better than Logan! I was firmly in the hands of Lucifer! I sinned in every imaginable way. Drugs, alcohol, wicked women!"

"Tell us about Kenny's Road House," requested Don.

"This was a wicked, wicked place! I saw the face of Satan there!"

"Oh, yeah," nodded Don. To an experienced television guy sightings of Satan were no big deal. "Tell us about the parking lot."

"I misunderstand, Donald. Parking lots are parking lots."

"But something happened in this one."

After a moment, Lindy nodded. "There was an accident."

"Logan was hit by a car. His knees got mangled."

Lindy nodded.

"How come Logan got hit by the car?"

Lindy muttered.

"Come again, Olver?"

"He was pushing me out of the way."

"It was *you* who was drunk and got in the way of the car. Logan pushed you to safety, then he got crunched. Right?"

Lindy nodded sagely. "The Lord works in mysterious ways."

Don smiled contentedly. He remembered his bargain and said, "It was my colleague Mickey Moonie who—hold on, hold on. Lemme get this straight. The Lord put Logan there just so's he could push you out of the way?"

"Who am I to question my Lord?"

"And now," Don said, his colour and voice rising, "you come here and try to score on Logan?"

"I have come to play hockey, yes, Donald."

"And and and," Don sputtered, "you come on 'Hockey Night in Canada' and call him a drunkard and a fornicator?"

"One of Satan's legions," Lindy added.

"Jesus Christ!" roared Don.

"Do not take His name in vain."

"Boy, Olver, are you ever a prick!"

The producer was having conniptions, but as it turned out, the interview was never used.

Eighteen

In the Falconbridge dressingroom, Big George Tyack was busily using an ionizer. He'd built it himself following a patent dated 1908. The purpose of the machine was to separate the positive and negative ions in the immediate atmosphere. This would create a highly charged air that the Falcons would find energizing. The ionizer looked a lot like a vacuum cleaner, so most of the players assumed that the coach was simply cleaning for some reason known best to himself.

Big George's research had also uncovered a connection between alien mindfuckers and the fabled Illuminati of the nineteenth century. Therefore, he had painted on the wall a large disembodied eye encased in a pyramid. Big George hoped that the Sirians would become confused and spend most of their time in the dressingroom communing with this image.

Leaving no bases untouched, Big George had appointed Joe Fineweather assistant coach. That man was standing in the middle of the floor chanting.

There came a knock on the dressingroom door and Big George went to shoo away whatever TV or newspaper person was daring to interrupt their preparations. However, the visitor turned out to be neither. He was an extremely sad-looking man, carefully cradling a hatbox. The man asked to speak to Logan, and approached him timidly.

"Hi."

Logan recognized him from the bus station.

"I met you at the place in South Grouse," said the sad man. There was something secretive in his tone. "I heard from a guy what was going on up here. So I thought maybe you might need this." The man stuck out the hatbox.

Logan lifted off the lid. Inside was a flying eagle.

"I didn't recognize you on the bus," the sad man apologized. "You looked like a bum."

Joe Fineweather saw the mask and came over emitting a series of giggles and guffaws. "Boy oh boy! We got them suckers by the short and curlies!"

Logan fitted the mask over his bruised and battered face.

"Remember now?" asked the sad man. "You gave it to me because you thought it might cheer me up."

"Yeah," said Logan inside the mask.

"My wife slept with my four best friends."

The flying eagle bobbed up and down.

"But really, you know," said the sad man, "it didn't have anything to do with my wife. I'm just a miserable guy. I guess that's likely why the missus did it."

"What you need," said Uncle Joe Fineweather, "is a protector."

"What's that?"

"A protector looks after you," explained Joe. "When a feeling of misery comes to you, your protector shoots the boots to it."

Something sparked inside the man's eyes. "How do I get one?"

Joe gesticulated for about three seconds. "You got one. And his name is . . ." Joe was really too excited. "Fred."

"I feel better already," announced the sad man. "Maybe I won't have to go back there no more."

∞   ∞   ∞

When Charlene Luttor saw Logan step onto the ice wearing his mask she laughed and clapped her hands. Things fell together in her mind like pieces of a jigsaw puzzle (suitable ages 3 – 147.) The pieces were things like good and bad, love and whatever her mother did with the men she brought home. There was even a piece with Mr. Greenjeans's face on it.

∞   ∞   ∞

Logan went to his crease. He began the sideways skating that would cut down the glare made worse by the many lights the CBC technicians had hung from the Coliseum's rafters.

Down at the other end, the Hope Blazers were taking shots at the kid. The crowd was applauding enthusiastically; Ridout was giving a spectacular display, looking like a bizarre cross between Johnny Bower and Rudolph Nureyev.

The crowd began to buzz. A golden-haired Hope player came dancing onto the ice. He took his warm-up circles at a dizzying clip and then charged toward a line of pucks. He picked one up on the blade of his stick and with a slap propelled it at Ridout. Bram went down into the splits, but the puck was already by him and nestled in the mesh.

"Sure, sure," muttered Logan.

Olver, having warmed up, came shooting down the ice. He arrived with one finger pointed upwards, a Born Again benediction. When he stopped he sprayed ice all over Logan. "God bless you, Logan."

"How's it hanging, Lindy-baby?"

Lindy Olver took a long time thinking about what to say next, which was, "No hard feelings?"

It struck Logan as an odd question. It occurred to him that most feelings were hard, or else why would they hurt so much when they were inside you? Logan shrugged and looked at the stands. The people of Falconbridge were cheering. The cameras from "Hockey Night in Canada" were pointed at

Lindy and himself. Logan almost laughed. "Aw, frig it, Lindy," he said, "it's just a hockey game."

Lindy offered his hands. "So, no hard feelings?"

Logan shook the hand. "The thing about it is, Lindy, you can't just *talk* one by me."

"True," agreed Lindy. Then he winked at Logan. At least, Logan was pretty sure Lindy winked at him. Lindy Olver turned to skate back to his own end.

"Hey, Lindy. I missed you, man."

Lindy skated away; Logan supposed he hadn't heard.

Kenny Pringle took to the ice. After some study Logan concluded that Pringle's perfectly round potbelly was nowhere to be seen. Logan recalled seeing the tummy the night before, so he reasoned that the man was trussed. Logan deemed it appropriate that the hockey game should be officiated by a man wearing a girdle.

Kenny Pringle dashed to centre ice and seemed about to toss the puck down, but then he stopped. He cocked his head attentively and Logan saw that he was wearing a little earphone. Pringle milled around, obviously awaiting some signal. Whatever it was came almost three minutes later. Pringle suddenly sprang into action, dashing the puck to the ice.

Lindy Olver won the opening face-off against Jay Fineweather. The puck went back to one of Lindy's linemates (not Jesus) and the linemate flipped it back up to Olver. Lindy came down the ice; he came quickly, and not a single Falcon managed to do anything about it. Olver stepped over the blue line and let loose a shot. Logan didn't know whether to stop it with a foot or a glove or a stick or what. As the replays would show, Logan wasn't even in the right neighbourhood. Logan swung stupidly with his stick and the puck went cruising by.

Olver raised his stick jubilantly and was about to drop to his knees when a loud, hollow *CLANG* rang through the Coliseum. Logan heard the crowd roar before he saw the puck come floating out. Olver saw the puck, too, and began a maniacal charge, but Logan smothered it with his glove.

Up in his booth, Dan was shouting, "Olver hit the post! He had Logan beat cleanly but he hit the post!" Dan kept waiting for Don to say something, but Don was saving himself for between periods and sleeping.

The next face-off was held to Logan's right. Olver let another Falcon take it and positioned himself in the slot area. The puck came back obediently and Olver took another shot. This one came marked for the upper corner. Logan didn't think about it; he reached with his trapper and pulled the puck out of the air.

∞   ∞   ∞

Bram Ridout's start was a trifle shaky as well. Bram caught a Jean-Guy Cabot slapshot imperfectly, almost losing it. That was his one moment of weakness.

On the other hand, Bram had several moments of brilliance. Most of them came against young Jay Fineweather, who was playing well, if a little nervously. All of the Falcons were playing good hockey, none more so than the four lads on defence. Stan the Man Huculak endeared himself to Logan by taking Lindy into the boards with a dull thud. It took Olver a few moments to become a scoring threat once more.

For all of his sermonizing and righteousness, Olver had the right attitude when it came to hockey. The boy enjoyed himself; there was wind in his style. The Falconbridge supporters couldn't help but applaud several of his feats. One they liked best was when Lindy appeared to skate *under* Parker Quinn's enormous legs. Logan might have enjoyed that one himself except that it left Lindy in the clear and twenty feet away. Olver cranked up, hesitated. He declined to shoot— nothing from that range had caused Logan too much of a problem—and elected instead to charge the net. And though it was foolhardy, Logan charged right back. Logan ploughed

167

into Olver, mowed him down. Logan spied the puck dribbling toward the unprotected net and swung at it, knocking it safely into the corner boards even as he sat upon Lindy Olver.

Olver laughed. "Logan, get up offa me."

Logan climbed off and genuflected. "Gorbless, bruvver."

"Okay, now," said Olver excitedly. "I'll go get the puck and I'll be right back. Okay?"

Lindy rushed off to get the puck. As soon as he touched it, Vic Pheresford and Faron Quinn both came at him. Lindy neatly stepped out of their way. The two biggest men in town hit each other with glorious conviction. As they stood erect, almost fused, Lindy reached his blade through their skates and drew the puck away. Then Pheresford and Quinn began the long crumple earthward.

Olver was in front of the net in no time. "Ta da!" he fanfared, and with a little pirouette he popped the puck at Logan. The puck was more shoved than shot, and it turned maddeningly, end over end. The sensible thing would be to gingerly smother the thing, so Logan turned a graceful pirouette of his own and plopped his keester over the puck. Logan heard Kenny Pringle's whistle and climbed to his feet.

The Falconbridge fans clapped only perfunctorily. Most of them felt Logan was going off the deep end, having watched his performance on "A Woman's Diary." Those who didn't care about his sanity were pissed off because Logan appeared to be farting around. Coast to coast television was never the best place to fart around. This attitude was best exemplified by Bram Ridout. He waited for a stoppage of play (for a Daisychains commercial) and then went skating up to his own blue line. Bram tore off the three-eyed lightning-filled mask. (Charlene Luttor was startled by his blond boyishness.)

"Logan!"

Logan tore off his flying eagle. "Yo, Brammy?"

"Will you please quit farting around?"

The request received much crowd support. The dissenters were likewise vocal with their boos, but there was a mere handful. Poor besotten Kristal was one, regaling Bram with a complicated series of obscene hand and finger gestures. Kristal felt ill because a) she'd consumed enough Birdbaths to bathe a treeful of birds and b) she had a vague misgiving that she was in love with Logan.

Charlene Luttor was also on Logan's side, and so was her mother, although Lottie did keep muttering, "Logan is farting around."

Logan's father was downright proud. "That's my baby boy!" he hollered, adding, "Not that everyone else isn't, too."

Logan's greatest supporter was Anthony O'Toole, because Anthony had sudden insight into this equation: hockey equals frozen rivers, wind and laughter.

"Tell you what, man." Olver wished he hadn't said *man*. It wasn't a Born Again thing to do. "I'll score on you, then we can have a nice long talk. I think you could find happiness in the Lord."

Kenny Pringle whistled Olver into the face-off circle.

"Do your damnedest, Lindy," said Logan.

Lindy took the face-off against Charlie Knowles. Charlie won it, because Lindy allowed him to. Knowles propelled the puck back and Lindy simply stepped over Charlie's stick and took possession. Lindy cranked up and smacked the puck for all he was worth. Logan caught it, returned it to the ice.

With about five minutes left in the period, Lars Løkan stood off to the side of Logan's net. Lars banged his stick and bellowed unintelligibly for the puck. The play moved down to the other end of the ice.

"Lars fak K−" Lars began.

"Yeah, yeah, yeah. Lars fak Kizzle. Big fucking deal."

"Ya," grinned Lars. Lars worked the shaft of his stick like a pool cue, digging it into Logan's stomach, pulling it back, leaving no evidence of wrongdoing except the bluishness of Logan's face. Logan swung his stick, bringing it up in a wide arc designed to decapitate Løkan. Løkan skated back, out of harm's way. Logan's stick stopped only when it met the crossbar on the way back down, jarring Logan enough that the beautiful eagle flew from his face. Logan was now wrenched around awkwardly, and his alien knees spied their chance. One, two, three, and the mindfuckers from the Dogstar pushed off in opposite directions. Logan pitched forward at the net. His forehead connected with the thick metal pipe. Logan felt something thick and warm running into his eyes, and he knew that he'd done fucked up again.

∞   ∞   ∞

Warren Bermondsey was eating a Joe Louis and washing it down with a Dr. Pepper. Warren had spent the afternoon at the Dove Hotel, where he'd done an inspired Logan imitation. He'd played pool badly and lost a lot of money betting on a basketball game. He'd told a filthy joke (actually, he'd confused two, so that his telling received only groans and raised eyebrows). His coup de grace came at about five-thirty, when he'd lunged at June the barmaid and sunk both hands into her bosom. Mostly he'd drunk beer, many quart bottles of Export, so by the time he wandered over to the Coliseum he was feeling quite vacant and dizzy.

Warren watched without interest as Logan talked with the big Danish defenceman. Mostly Warren was remembering June's breasts, which reminded him of clouds. Warren was marginally alarmed when Logan took a roundhouse swing at the guy, because if Pringle saw it there'd be a penalty for sure. The infraction, fortunately, went unnoticed. Warren tried to imagine June naked, pink clouds with nipples and pubic hair. Warren giggled when Logan missed, lost his mask and fell over.

When Warren saw Logan's face turn a bright crimson he got worried.

∞   ∞   ∞

The gash was about an inch and a half long. It didn't hurt much, and it wasn't all that deep, but it did release what seemed like buckets of blood. Logan's face and jersey were slick with the stuff. He was blinded, blood pouring into his eyes quicker than he could wipe them clean. Kenny Pringle looked at the cut for a moment or two and said, "Get it stitched."

"It's gonna stop bleeding soon," protested Logan.

"Come on." Kenny Pringle began to pull Logan toward the Falconbridge bench. The coach was waiting with needle and thread.

"Hey, Pringle," said Logan (Logan couldn't see anything, not even the referee two feet in front), "this won't take long. Five, six stitches tops. How long could that take?"

"It's on television," whispered Kenny. "This is 'Hockey Night in Canada.'"

"I know. That's why—"

"That's why we can't keep the nation waiting while you get stitched."

"Jesus, Ken, you can't—" Logan wiped out his eyes just in time to see Kenny Pringle motion for Warren Bermondsey to take over the Falconbridge net.

And a soft murmur swept through the Coliseum. "Oh oh."

Even Dan said "Oh oh." He went on, "The Falcons appear to be substituting young Warren Bermondsey while Logan gets some medical attention."

Don woke up to say, "Oh oh."

Logan sat down on the bench disgusted. Big George Tyack attended to him with the hands of a midwife.

The Falcons were, according to OPHL rules, allowed two minutes to warm up Warren. Then Warren would be obliged to remain in net for at least one play, from face-off to next whistle. Logan would be stitched in plenty of time to get back, but by then it could be too late. Warren's style was that of a flopper, except in his case it was more of a tripper or an

I-couldn't-stay-on-my-feet-if-I-was-paider style. Once Logan's eyes were clear of blood, he stared at Warren very sadly indeed. Then he thought of something.

"Joe."

Joe Fineweather was standing some feet away. His arms were crossed over his chest and he was staring at the Falconbridge crowd in a bemused way.

"Joe!" Logan repeated.

"Yes, Logan?"

Logan didn't notice the stitching needle being driven through his skin. Logan said to Joe, "Give him a yahoo!"

"I beg your pardon?"

"You know, a thing." Logan pointed at his own shoulder. "A yahoo. A papu. A fred. A . . . ." Logan snapped his fingers. "A protector."

"What, you think I go around *giving* those things away?"

"Yes!" shouted Logan. "Don't you?"

Warren's two-minute warm-up was drawing to an end. Kenny Pringle had the puck in his hand and was skating for the face-off circle just to Warren's right. Standing at the rim of the circle, grinning in a very un-Christian manner, was Lindy Olver.

"Give him one!" shouted Logan.

"It's not that easy."

"Bullshit," said Logan, just as Big George clipped the last suture. Logan jumped to his feet and stomped over to Joe. "I seen you do it. All you do is wave your hands in the air. So give one to Warren!"

"I'll tell you what. You think it's so easy, you give him one."

"Huh?"

"Give him Yahoo."

"Give him Yahoo? Then who'll look after me?"

"Then you'll have to look after yourself." Joe pointed toward the ice. "Kenneth is going to recommence the game."

"I don't know if I want to give him Yahoo."

"I know you don't, Logan. That's why Warren doesn't have a protector."

Logan gazed at the face-off circle. He studied his old friend Lindy. "How do I do it?"

"Wave your hands in the air."

"Come on."

"It's true, Logan."

Logan waved his hands in the air.

"Uh-uh," said Joe Fineweather.

"How come?"

"You didn't open your heart to him."

"Uncle Joe, we don't have time for this garbage."

"It's what you have to do," said Joe, just as Pringle threw the puck to the ice. "Your heart is a little moron sitting in a corner whacking off. For this to work it has to get involved."

Lindy Olver, back at the blue line, was cranking up for a shot.

Logan tried to open his heart to Warren Bermondsey.

Lindy Olver smacked the puck for all he was worth.

The puck flew toward Warren's right shoulder. Warren moved to deflect it, but the puck was coming too quickly and his beer-drenched reflexes were far too slow. The puck flew over Warren's shoulder.

A moment later, the puck was in front of Warren once more. Big Warren was in the act of falling over anyway, and his girth smothered the puck very effectively.

Pringle whistled the play dead.

Big George Tyack stared at the net. "What happened?"

Logan grinned a Fineweather grin. "Must have hit the crossbar, Coach."

Big George shook his head. "I didn't see it hit no crossbar."

Up in the makeshift broadcast booth, Dan hadn't seen the puck bounce off any crossbar either. Dan asked the executive producer for an instant replay. The producer informed him that something had gone wrong with the instant playback machine. It had devoured the play in question.

Dan shrugged, although inwardly he was upset. Dan had wanted to watch the replay just to convince himself that he hadn't seen the puck bounce off something that looked like a bird with fur and pointy teeth.

Nineteen

Don and Dan were going over the scanty biographical information they had on Logan. They suspected that the research department had acquired what bumf they had from a Marshall's Instant Pudding Coin.

"Somebody must know something about him!" shrieked Don.

King McGee happened to be sitting in the control booth, rubbing shoulders with the boys from the big city, hoping to impress them with the Messianic timbre of his voice. Don and Dan had ignored King for the most part, although Don (usually the friendlier of the two) had earlier sent the boy out for a bottle of rye. King McGee now said, "I KNOW SOMETHING ABOUT LOGAN," and could not be ignored.

The horn went to end the (sixteenth) period. Don and Dan didn't have any time to appraise McGee's proclaimed information. They stuck him in a chair and began the interview.

"Here's a young man who can tell us some of Logan's colourful history," said Don. "And you are –?"

"KINGSLEY McGEE," said Kingsley McGee, in his absolute best possible voice. It filled the room magically. Don and Dan took a nervous glance upwards and then stared at McGee with something resembling awe. "I'M THE ANCHORPERSON AT THE CWCO, THE VOICE OF FALCONBRIDGE, ONTARIO."

The producer was staring at King McGee, too. Don and Dan wished they weren't so snoozled.

"How do you know Logan, King?" Don demanded in a crisp, even tenor.

"WELL, DON, LOGAN AND I GREW UP TOGETHER. WE'RE BOTH FROM THE SAME HOME TOWN."

Don stole a glance at the Logan fact-sheet. "That would be South Grouse, Ontario?"

"YES, IT WOULD. WE ARE BOTH SOUTH GROUSERS."

Dan suddenly leant forward with an interjection. "And just where is *North* Grouse?"

Don and the producer both frowned heavily.

"THERE IS NO SUCH PLACE. JUST A SOUTH GROUSE."

"Were you and Logan friends?" asked Don in a clipped, professional manner.

"LOGAN IS THREE YEARS OLDER THAN I, SO WE DID NOT PLAY TOGETHER. I WAS NOT ALLOWED NEAR HIS HOME. THAT IS TO SAY, WHERE HE LIVED. BUT I KNEW HIM."

"How so?" asked Don—succinct, terse, methodical.

"BECAUSE HE WAS A LOGAN. EVERYONE IN SOUTH GROUSE KNEW THE LOGANS."

"And why might that be?"

"BECAUSE THEY WERE NUTS," recalled King McGee. "ABSOLUTELY STARK RAVING MAD, EVERY LAST ONE OF THEM."

∞   ∞   ∞

The atmosphere in the Falconbridge dressingroom was heavy, all of the players glumly readjusting equipment. Big George Tyack was staring with disgust at the disembodied eye he had rendered upon the wall.

The only bright spark was Logan. He stood in the middle of the room doing an impersonation of Perry Como, not that anybody recognized it as such or gave a damn. Logan ran through a few standards before launching nonchalantly into "Try to Remember." Then his voice became strangely choked and he covered his face with the flying eagle mask.

Big George blamed himself, of course. The way he figured, the floating eye had attracted mindfuckers from every corner of the universe (not that Big George believed that the universe had corners). But now the coach's problem was: should he leave the eye there (with the Sirians arriving like moths to a light bulb) or should he wash it away (thereby loosing the already accumulated into the Coliseum proper)?

Big George was about to confide his troubles to Logan when he remembered that he had an envelope in his pocket addressed to the goaltender. He pulled it out and handed it to Logan.

"What's this now?" asked Logan. "An offer from the Toronto Maple Leafs? Well, they can get stuffed. I wouldn't leave my buddies in Falconbridge for nothing." Logan looked at the letterhead and shut up. He headed for free bench space and plopped himself down heavily. Logan tore the envelope open, read the contents, and then dropped both to the floor.

"Good news?" asked Uncle Joe Fineweather.

Logan snapped out of whatever it was. "Yeah! Great news. My family's here."

The Falconbridge Falcons demanded, "Your family?"

"Sure. A guy's got a family, right? Why wouldn't I have a family?"

His teammates shrugged, although many seemed far from convinced.

Jean-Guy Cabot, who despite his demonic tactics on the ice was as sentimental as they come, said, "They must be of you very proud."

Logan nodded slowly. "I just bet they are."

∞   ∞   ∞

About eleven minutes into the next period, Kenny Pringle assessed what everyone agreed was one dumb-ass penalty.

Specifically, he called Falconbridge's Theodore Carney for tripping. The replay showed that Ted was singlemindedly after the puck and had no intention of interfering with the Hope player. More than that, the Hope player's tumble was so obviously a dive that he should have swum away. The crowd hurled abuse upon Kenny Pringle. One old Falconbridge geezer even sacrificed his bifocals, hurling them to the ice, shouting, "Wear these, you mealy-eyed prick!" Pringle ignored them all.

Just before the play in question (which was down at the other end) Logan had been watching the referee. Pringle seemed to be vibrating, like the low string on a double-bass. Then, suddenly, Pringle's perfectly round potbelly exploded underneath his black and white jersey. Pringle instantly went beet-red and blew his whistle. Everyone stared, bewildered as to why the play had been stopped. There was no signal to signify stoppage due to a busted girdle, so Pringle made a tripping motion and pointed at Ted Carney.

Pringle's belly vanished, but not the beet-red colouring. Kenny intended to referee the rest of the game with his gut sucked up out of sight. Logan wondered if Pringle would survive.

Before play could be resumed, Big George Tyack had to have one of his tantrums. The crowd loved these. First the coach leapt up onto the players' bench. He unleashed a torrent of hexes and curses, running the gamut from ancient Greek to modern Shashone. Big George was so distraught that he even used some of Alastair Crowley's black magicks, etching invisible stars onto his palms and making the secret invocations that would summon the Beast 666.

Ordinarily Pringle would have ranted and raved right back. This time he merely skated over to Tyack and asked him in a curiously strangled manner to stop.

Big George sent out his penalty killing squad, three defencemen and Jay Fineweather. This may have been a tactical error; Jay was exhausted, dripping with sweat.

Lindy Olver, on the other hand, had been resting on the Hope bench for the past two shifts. As he jumped over the boards, Logan recognized something in Olver's blue-grey eyes: a twisted sparkling.

Lindy spent a long time positioning his teammates. It was as if he had precognition, so precise were his instructions. Then Lindy went to the face-off circle and hunkered over.

It was like a checker move, the kind where one man jumps five or six opponents and then kings itself. Olver won the face-off, propelling it backwards to Lars Løkan. Lars flipped it to the man standing by the right boards. Et cetera. Lindy leisurely skated down the ice toward Logan; he received the puck without seeming to look for it. Olver took a wristshot, a quick motion like a serpent's tongue.

Logan hurled himself sideways, the only chance he had. The puck hit the webbing of his glove. For a moment, Logan was sure that he had it. Then, in slow motion, Logan watched the puck pop out. Logan fell onto his back and swatted at the puck with his stick; again, he thought he had it. But when he heard the sickly little *tick* (all was silence in the Coliseum), Logan knew he'd missed by a fraction of an inch. All he'd done was steer the puck even more surely toward his net. Logan rolled over to witness his defeat.

Something flew over his head. Logan knew without seeing that it was Jay Fineweather. Jay flew like Superman, his arms stretched out in front. Jay landed in the crease, an awkward landing like a dodo's, his face meeting the ice, his bones smacking with brittle clicks.

No goal light came on. A whistle sounded. Jay climbed awkwardly to his knees. Logan stared at Jay's hand, which held the puck.

Jay looked down; the sight of his own hand alarmed him. He muttered, "Oh, shit."

Up in the stands, Anthony O'Toole considered saying "Oh, shit" but opted for "Oh, spot and bother!" so as not to alarm his mother.

179

"What's the matter?" asked Mrs. O'Toole. "He stopped the puck, didn't he?"

"Yes, but—" Little Anthony hesitated. There was still a chance that Kenny Pringle wouldn't make the correct call.

Logan and Jay were hoping for the same thing. Jay opened his hand gingerly and let the puck fall to the ice.

Dan told his listeners, "This could be a—" then he too fell silent. No one was going to help Kenny Pringle.

Pringle scooped up the puck, scratched his head and said, "Oh, yeah. Penalty shot."

There were many, many groans.

∞   ∞   ∞

From the official OPHL rulebook:

> Rule 54: a) any infraction of the rules which calls for a penalty shot shall be taken as follows: the referee shall cause to be announced over the public address system the name of the player designated by him to take the shot.

Kenny Pringle consulted the little rulebook and furrowed his brow. It was easy to designate the player—it was Lindy Olver's shot that Fineweather had interfered with—but Pringle had no idea how to cause that to be announced on the public address system, because there wasn't any such thing in the Coliseum. Pringle considered bellowing the name at the top of his voice, but then he would lose the internal retention of his potbelly. Kenny Pringle looked up at the control booth that contained Don and Dan from "Hockey Night in Canada." He pointed a finger at Lindy Olver and smiled hopefully. Just when he thought they'd paid him no attention, a voice rang out of nowhere.

"PENALTY SHOT TO BE TAKEN BY NUMBER 9, LINDY OLVER."

A great fan of "Hockey Night in Canada," Pringle did not

recognize the voice as belonging to either Don or Dan. Indeed, it sounded . . .

Pringle turned back to his rulebook. Foolishness, he told himself. Kenny was a Church-going, God-fearing man, who reckoned the Lord had better things to do than make announcements at hockey games.

b) While the penalty shot is being taken, players of both sides shall withdraw to the sides of the rink and beyond the centre red line.

Pringle corralled the players with flamboyant sweeps of his arms, knowing the television camera was riveted to him.

c) The referee shall place the puck on the centre face-off spot and the player taking the penalty shot will, on the referee's instruction, play the puck from there and attempt to score on the goalkeeper. The player taking the shot may carry the puck in any part of the neutral zone or his own defending zone, but once the puck has crossed the Attacking Blue Line it must be kept in motion toward the opponents' goal line and once the puck is shot the play shall be considered complete.

Memories clung to Lindy Olver the way twigs, leaves and dirt cling to an old dog.

Lindy had once kicked in a girlfriend's teeth, uppers and lowers. He'd been enormously drunk, amphetamine-crazed. He'd watched the heel of his boot meet the girl's mouth and marvelled at how easily the teeth came out. That was just—simply—one of his memories. Other memories, hundreds of them, didn't differ substantially.

Lindy started behind his own net.

Another memory: Logan getting hit by the car. Logan laughing as he flew through the air, too drunk to realize he'd been hurt. Lindy's conversion hadn't come until a year later,

181

but it was that night, really, that he had discovered God. Or had discovered at least that God meant to get him, no matter what—a discovery that sickened Olver until he made his uneasy truce with the Man's boy, Jesus.

Lindy Olver skated for the puck at centre ice, faster and faster, so the wind would make memories disappear. Fast enough so that only a lonely one would be strong enough to cling to him.

Lindy in his snowsuit, Lindy in his mittens. Lindy skating in the back yard while his parents laughed inside the warm house. Lindy with the dead trees, Lindy on the star-filled ice, Lindy in the little world.

When he picked up the puck at centre ice, even that memory flew away.

d) The goalkeeper must remain in his crease until the player taking the penalty shot has touched the puck. The goalkeeper may attempt to stop the shot in any manner except by throwing his stick or any object.

Logan, on the other hand, collected memories the way an old crazy man collects newspapers in plastic bags. When he needed strength, Logan would take them out and look at them. Kristal laughing in the bed was one of his favourites. Logan pulled out that one and looked, leaving only part of him to watch Lindy Olver come skating down the ice.

For a moment (when Lindy was halfway to him and Logan began to move out) life was simple.

Then Lindy shot the puck, and life wasn't simple anymore.

∞   ∞   ∞

"Let's watch that again in slow motion!" shouted Dan.

Don scowled. It was the sixth time they'd watched it in slow motion. Their jobs were on the line (especially with that King

McGod wandering around) and they could ill-afford to be watching things over and over again in slow motion.

"This," Dan told his listeners, "is exciting. Breathtaking. Spine-tingling!"

They turned once again to the monitor. That little screen showed nothing but two men playing hockey.

The two men in question had seen other things.

Logan was certain that he'd seen a little blond boy in a snowsuit come barrelling down the ice, splay-footed and cross-eyed with concentration.

Lindy Olver (although he never told a soul) was sure that he'd seen a naked woman sitting in a bed and laughing with all of her being.

All the screen showed was one man shooting the puck and the other man falling to the ice sideways, kicking out with a long leg.

It also showed the puck bouncing off the goaltender's shinpad.

The puck bounced very high in the air and turned for what seemed like forever. It was finally caught, high in the stands, by little Anthony O'Toole.

∞   ∞   ∞

Logan's stop seemed to infuse the other Falcons with high-powered adrenalin. Jean-Guy Cabot jumped over the boards with his blood boiling audibly. At 16:07 of the period, Jean-Guy and Jay Fineweather went down the ice. The Hope defence got caught on a line change and the Falconbridge duo found themselves with a two-on-one. The lone defender stayed with Jay, so Jay slipped the puck across ice at the moment Jean-Guy started to crank. The timing was perfect. The stick met the puck with an ear-splitting crack.

There seemed to be nothing Bram Ridout could do about it.

The Falconbridge fans opened their mouths, intending to cheer.

Logan's father, quite forgetting himself, clapped his hands together with excitement.

Then everything was darkness.

Twenty

When the storm finally hit, it hit hard. It knocked out the power almost effortlessly, batting hydro towers and telephone poles to the ground. There was great confusion in the Coliseum, but the people finally realized what was happening and began a reasonably methodical evacuation.

Many people went to the Dove Hotel. (The sign, by the way, the strange misshapen bird, had disappeared, blown away by the winds.) The CBC technicians had generators to light the room, although there was no way to sustain the refrigeration system. It was Logan who suggested that the beer might go bad so they might as well drink it all that night.

Logan was the first person to the Dove. He'd torn off his uniform in pitch-darkness and jumped into his street clothes. He was sweaty and smelly and likely crawling with little creatures, but all that seemed fair somehow.

Coach George Tyack came in along with Jay and Joe Fineweather. Their mood was basically good, except for Uncle Joe, who claimed to be "under the weather." Joe kept saying, "I knew it was up to something. And *you* —" He'd point at Big George accusingly. "You, wasting your time on those guys from the Dogstar Sirius. You know what? I bet every time something goes wrong up there they say 'Mindfuckers from the Planet Earth!' "

Dr. Bermondsey entered with his charges. Logan went

quietly to join them. They sat at one of the Dove's little round tables. Logan wished that Kristal was there beside him.

Dr. Bermondsey said, "Well done, Logan. What splendid reflexes you have."

Logan's father, dressed in his starfield robes, sobbed miserably. "I'm sorry, son. I forgot Myself." Logan's father was producing tears at an alarming rate. There was a distinct family resemblance.

Logan's mother was a shrivelled and fairly nasty old woman. She fit right in at the Dove Hotel. Dr. Bermondsey allowed her one glass of draught beer. Logan's mother, Edna by name, poured it down her throat and became instantly pissed. (Again we see genetics at work.) Edna pointed an arthritic finger at Logan's face. "What the heck happened to you?"

Logan ignored the question. "How are you, Mommy?"

Edna Logan searched for impromptu weaponry.

Logan's brother Pluto broke into song. *"Raindrops keep falling on my head—"*

"Did you notice," said Dr. Bermondsey, reaching for a little notepad he carried with him, "the number of nervous tics and mannerisms that young Ridout has?" Dr. Bermondsey flipped through five or six pages' worth.

Lindy Olver entered the bar. He was probably on a soul-saving mission, but to Logan he had the old cruising look to him. Logan's sister Neptunia (Neppy, for short) attempted a seductive grin. Her middle linebacker's physique made it quite the stunt. "Isn't Lindy Olver attractive?" she asked in a conversational way. "I'd like to give him a—"

"Neptunia," cautioned Dr. Bermondsey.

"—great big kiss on the cheek!" Neppy finished innocently.

Kristal Donahue entered the bar, unseen by Logan. She was hung over and weary. She climbed aboard a barstool and sighed.

Logan's mother Edna poked a bended finger into her son's face. "Are you married?"

"No."

"Is she nice?"

Pluto began to sing "Feelings."

Logan looked around the Dove Hotel. He'd never seen it so crowded. All the Falcons and all the Hope Blazers were there. Everyone was in the kind of good mood that comes from being warm and dry when a hellish storm is raging in the world outside. The two teams were holding boat races, relay beer-guzzling battles. Logan wished that he could join his team. (They wished he could, too; he was their anchorman.)

Pluto kicked his chair backwards and stood up from the table. *"Feelings . . . oh, oh, oh, feelings . . ."*

Lindy Olver was sitting by himself at a table; he appeared to be praying.

Uncle Joe Fineweather was doing some anti-storm chanting. It clashed bizarrely with Pluto's silky lounge stylings.

Jay was talking with Laurie Fredericks.

Don and Dan were sound asleep, although every so often one or the other would wake up with a start and order more drinks.

Bram Ridout was turning green because of all the ale he was drinking in the boat race.

King McGee was sitting at a table with Darla Featherstone, the perfect weather/social calendar woman, and the producer of "Hockey Night in Canada." The producer was paying for all their drinks.

Anthony O'Toole was sitting at a table with his mother. Ordinarily, little Anthony would not have been allowed inside the Dove, but circumstances were far from ordinary. Anthony's mother was chatting warmly with a man who was either or neither Buck Tanager or Elmore Daisy. Which is to say, that person was halfway through changing persona when the black-out came.

Most of the people in the Dove were listening to Pluto Logan sing "Feelings." When he dropped to one knee for the big finish they burst into applause.

Logan excused himself, went to buy a drink. He squeezed in

at the bar and gestured irritably. Logan heard a voice saying, "Hi."

Logan hadn't talked to Kristal since the night he'd been so smashed at Birds of a Feather, and that hadn't been one of the all-time great conversations. Logan's emotions mixed up a mulligan's stew and made speech impossible.

"One hell of a game," noted Kristal. "The game of your life."

Logan managed to say, "You want a drink?" because the bartender had arrived.

Kristal shrugged. "Maybe a beer."

"Couple of beer," Logan said, "and a –" Logan looked briefly at Kristal. "Just a couple of beer, thanks."

They stood silently and waited for the drinks. The bartender set them down and asked, "What do you figure? You figure that last shot was a goal or what?"

A lot of people were talking about Jean-Guy's shot and whether it went into the net. "I would wager with you the universe and its contents!" said Cabot, the author of the shot. The only person who knew for sure was Bram Ridout, who excused himself from the boat race and charged for the Dove's washroom. Logan no longer cared.

"Who are those people?" asked Kristal.

Logan knew who she meant. "So, um, you slept with that big Danish goom, did you?"

Logan and Kristal both turned to their beers.

"It's your family, isn't it? And you don't even think I might want to meet them?"

"Why would you want to meet them?"

"Shit for brains," muttered Kristal.

The crowd demanded another tune. "Thank you, ladies and gentlemen," said Pluto smoothly. "Here's one for anybody who's in love tonight." Pluto wandered over to a young woman and shot her a smouldering look. "*You look to me like misty roses . . .*"

"Yeah, it's my family," said Logan. "That's Pluto. And that

girl there" — Logan jerked his thumb at the table — "is my sister, Neppy. Neptunia. That's my mother and father."

Kristal asked, "What's your name, Logan?"

"What do you mean?"

"I mean, what's your name? Your given name?"

Logan looked confused. "You know my name."

Now Kristal looked confused. "How the hell would I know?"

"Search me. But you called me by it."

"What?" Kristal remembered back. "Mars."

"Not so loud."

"Mars is the most beautiful name in the world. I wish you'd told me sooner."

"Well, now you know."

"Now may be too late."

Logan finished his beer. "Maybe."

Kristal Donahue stared at Mars Logan evenly. "What's this? Some apeshit thing to do with Lars?"

"Lars. Now *there's* a dumb name."

"You're a dickhead, Mars. I take it that if I stay here we're going to have a great big heavy."

Logan considered it. "I suppose."

"Well, then, I'm off." Kristal dismounted and saluted Logan. "See you later."

"Goodbye," mumbled Logan, and then Kristal left.

I am a dickhead, thought Mars Logan.

Logan drank heavily, but his body had come up with a cagey and magical new way of dealing with the stuff: every mouthful made Logan feel emptier and emptier. All Logan's dreams, good and bad, were drinking at the Dove Hotel.

Logan puzzled over the complexity of his heart.

Logan tried to pretend he was a simple man. He pretended that he had a wife and family and blessings to count on his fingers. Logan pretended that his only problem was that his faithful old sheepdog, Belvedere, had dug up the neighbour's petunias. Logan pretended that the bottle of beer in his hand was a reward for work, compensation for the sweat on his brow. Logan pretended that on a clear night he could see all the gods in the sky.

∞ ∞ ∞

Through sheer perseverance and doggedness, Logan got drunk. It was not a very comfortable sort of intoxication, it was muzzy and elephantine, although it has historical significance: it was the last time Logan ever got drunk.

At one point, Jay Fineweather came up and asked Logan to keep an eye on his Uncle Joe. Apparently Jay was going somewhere with Laurie Fredericks. Logan nodded and routinely pinched the girl's bottom. "Ouch," said Jay as he led the girl away.

Logan decided to behave badly. Everyone at the Dove was pickled, so no one paid him much attention. Among other things, Logan kissed Lindy Olver on the lips and poured a jug of beer onto Bram Ridout's lap. He was hoping young Bram would knock him senseless, but Bram was greenly dry-heaving. Logan woke up Don and Dan and insulted them on a professional level. He mooned King McGee. He tweaked Darla's bosom. Logan stole the Stetson from Buck Daisy's head and ran for the little stage. He jumped onto it and began to sing country-and-western songs. Logan was about to launch into a striptease when something began to bother him.

Logan raised his hands into the air, demanding attention.

"Hey!" cried Logan. "Does anybody know where Joe Fineweather is?"

The patrons either shrugged or shook their heads.

"Oh oh." Logan jumped off the stage and headed for the front door. Lindy Olver intercepted him.

"Where are you going, Logan?" he asked.

"Gotta go find Joe."

"Logey, you can't go outside. Come on over here and sit down."

"Fuck you, Lindy." Logan pushed Olver away.

"You're drunk," said Lindy.

Logan hit Olver with all of his might. It was a besotten, ill-aimed punch. Logan was aiming for something relatively harmless, near the chest, but he connected with Lindy's nose. Olver went sprawling backwards, spewing blood.

Logan pushed through the front door. It took all of his strength to open it against the wind, but Logan escaped into the storm.

∞   ∞   ∞

Ice storms are something God came up with when He was in a particularly foul mood. God realized that they were so gruesome He couldn't really make much use of them, so He limited their employment to the Arctic, selected mountaintops, and Ontario.

The world outside the Dove Hotel was coated with ice, a dark blue crust that made everything treacherous. The wind raged near hurricane level. Logan fell down hard and the wind pushed him thirty or forty feet along the street. Logan managed to grab hold of a fire hydrant, but by then he was lost. Logan could see nothing but silver needles. The wind had spun him around, knocking out any sense of direction. Logan searched frantically for a landmark.

Lightning lit the sky. Logan could see the silhouette of Falconbridge. To his left he saw the shape of the tall radio tower stabbing toward the clouds. Logan saw a small shape about halfway up it.

Logan struggled to his feet and fell over again. He was carried farther down the street and then hit something hard. Logan waited for another flash of lightning so that he could get his bearings. He had arrived at the doorstep of Li's Hardware. Logan pulled himself to his feet, huddled in the corner and wondered what to do.

Logan realized that if he simply abandoned himself to the

wind he would be carried northward, toward the Coliseum. He yanked up his sweater over his head and stepped out. He managed to stay upright for a good many feet before he was bowled over. Logan flipped onto his back and allowed himself to be pushed. He rolled across the curb and then crawled forward. He was soon at the front door of the Coliseum. Logan pulled off one of his boots and knocked out a plate of glass. He reached through (carving a thick gash into his forearm) and unlatched the door.

It was mercifully peaceful inside the arena, and much of Logan was tempted to sleep. He allowed himself some ten seconds of rest, then stood up. The darkness inside the Coliseum was total, but Logan knew his way well. He put his right hand out to find the wall and quickly and surely guided himself to the dressingroom. It was a simple matter to find his own locker.

∞ ∞ ∞

Logan put on his entire uniform; the padding would break the many falls he was about to take. He put on the flying eagle mask for protection against the needles of ice. He took his stick for balance. He laced on his skates.

Logan returned to the world outside.

Logan placed the blade of his stick on the ground and leant his weight against it. He pushed with his skates. He thanked God (or whomever) that he'd had his skates sharpened that night, because the blades bit easily into the silver-blue crust. Logan found that he was moving forward, against the raging wind. Sometimes an erratic gust from the side would knock him over, but Logan discovered he could prevent himself from sliding too much by spreadeagling. He could pull himself upwards on the shaft of his stick and continue toward the radio station.

Lightning filled the sky every few seconds, so Logan could

check his direction. He could also see the tiny figure moving ever higher on the tower. Sometimes in the flash of light Logan could see a fist raised against the storm.

As the figure moved nearer the top, Logan pushed harder. Every step burned in his knees like a branding iron. Logan pushed against the wind, against the storm, against the world, and when he thought he could push no more Logan fell through the door of the radio station.

Logan abandoned his stick and skates and groped blindly for the staircase. He began to climb. About halfway one of his knees gave out and Logan tumbled down a flight. He pulled himself then, using the bannister as a handhold, because the knee was wobbly and unsteady. Fortunately the fall seemed to have numbed it.

At the top of the staircase was the door to the roof. The wind pushed against it so strongly that Logan could open it only a quarter of an inch and then only for a brief moment. Logan moved backwards on the landing and ran. He flew into the air, twisting himself sideways, and his shoulder pad met the wood. Then came an instant of pain, so hot and intense that Logan fainted.

The needles of ice revived him. Logan lay on the rooftop. A dagger of lightning showed him that Uncle Joe had reached the tower's summit. Joe was bellowing at the darkness, shaking a fist at the lunatic night. Logan crawled to the base of the tower and began to pull himself skyward.

"Joe!" Logan screamed. The wind carried the sound away mischievously, leaving behind only the howl of the wind.

Logan dropped his gloves so that his grip on the tower was more sure. Every hold froze instantly to the metal and Logan had to rip it away. Soon his palms were slick with blood.

Joe Fineweather bellowed to the night, "Fuck you!"

"Joe!" Logan screamed. "Joe! Come down!" Somehow it carried. Joe Fineweather looked down from his perch and smiled gently. "Hello, Logan! Fancy meeting you here!"

"Come on down, now!"

"I won't come down until it promises to stop!" hollered Joe. He shook his fist, cursed loudly to the skies.

"It won't stop until you come down!"

This seemed to make sense to Joe. "Like a truce?"

"Like a truce!" agreed Logan.

Joe pondered this, sitting at the top of the tower. Despite the winds and daggers of ice, Joe seemed quite comfortable. "Well, maybe," he decided.

"Come down, now!" shouted Logan once more.

"There's your friend," Joe pointed out. Logan twisted around, looked downward, but could see nothing.

"Come down, Joe!" shouted Logan.

Joe Fineweather turned to the heart of the storm. "What do you say? Let's make a truce!"

A bolt of lightning slapped Joe Fineweather off the tower.

Logan was thrown backwards.

"Logan!" someone screamed.

Logan's fall was broken, but he'd passed out long before he neared the rooftop.

Not long after, the storm left the earth.

THE LAST DAY

Twenty-one

The physician at the Lewiston General Hospital was a nice young man. He explained very softly to Jay Fineweather that there had been nothing they could do for his uncle. It was likely painless. Lightning doesn't burn or char for the most part, the doctor explained, rather it short-circuits the heart. Jay nodded. Big George Tyack placed one of his immense hands on Jay's shoulder.

"What about Logan?" asked the coach.

"Mr. Logan is, by and large, fine. He has a few cuts and bruises, and we're treating him for exposure. But, all considered, he's a fortunate man."

"And," asked Big George, "how's Lindy Olver?"

The doctor shrugged kindly. "Hard to say. He's a young man, in excellent health, so we have every reason to believe that he'll mend. But that sort of injury—I mean, an injury to the legs and spinal cord—is very unpredictable."

Mickey Moonie was standing nearby, writing down this latest scoop. "Let me get this straight. Olver tried to *catch* Logan?"

The doctor spread his hands, hesitant to commit himself. "So it would appear."

There was another man, a stranger, in the corridor. He approached the young doctor shyly, asked after Mars Logan.

"Mars?" wondered Jay Fineweather.

"Er, yes," nodded the man. "His father has long been fascinated with bodies astronomical."

Mickey Moonie elbowed people out of the way, drawing out her notepad and licking her pencil. "What do you know about all this?" she snapped.

"Well," said the man, "quite a bit. I'm Dr. Louis Bermondsey. Director of the South Grouse Home for Mental Health."

Big George Tyack shot Dr. Bermondsey a withering look. "Are you gonna tell us that Logan is mental?"

The man shook his head emphatically, drew out a pipe. "No. Not mental at all."

"Spit it out. Cough it up," Mickey Moonie snapped.

Dr. Louis Bermondsey spent a few moments attempting to get his Meerschaum smoking. His words came out in little puffs. "Very well. I will confess that this is all, to a degree, my fault. But place yourself in my position. I was confronted with a family of five, four of whom had drastic problems. I had never published, had no hope of professional advancement, until I thought, what if I did not break up the family? What if the fifth member of the family, the young boy, should live with his family, at the mental hospital? I could—and did—monitor his progress. I could—and did—publish a monograph. I can—and will—tell you the results."

"Yo," shot Mickey Moonie.

Dr. Bermondsey took his hands and placed fingertips together. "He's got a hole in his heart about the size of a hockey puck."

∞   ∞   ∞

Logan's dream went like this.

Zortron (who, not entirely coincidentally, hails from the Dogstar Sirius) launched a very savage attack against our little blue world. His first campaign was to send a storm of meteorites. The rocks fell to earth slowly, and trees pushed up from the ground to catch them. The trees were under the command of a little boy who dressed strangely. The boy sat on a high limb of the mightiest oak and giggled furiously. Some of the smaller stones from the sky (those about the size of a hockey puck) fell through the branches toward the ground. On the ground were Mars Logan and Bram Ridout, suited-up in their hockey gear, their faces covered with painted shields. Neither was about to let a single meteorite by. In Logan's dream, Yahoo was visible. Yahoo looked quite a bit like Koko, the military cockatoo from Birds of a Feather, except that Yahoo had a human face. Yahoo was a dead ringer for Uncle Joe Fineweather. At any rate, between Logan, Bram and the boy in the trees, Zortron couldn't even put through a pebble. "All right, all right. Geez. Enough with meteors. But how about a little time monkey business?" Zortron filled the world with lunatic laughter.

Time monkey business was strange. Everyone kept falling through black holes. Inside the black hole, you were both a child and an old man. Zortron took advantage of the ensuing confusion by sending an armada of lunarsailers. Our little blue world was doomed. The little boy Logan and the old man Logan watched the huge sails in the sky.

"All your fault!" The old man Logan used his cane to whack the little boy Logan's backside.

"Up yours," snorted the little boy Logan. "Useless old fart."

Mountains pushed out of the earth. The lunarsailers crumpled against them like candy-bar wrappers.

"Oy," groaned Zortron. "Look. Just send me that guy Logan. We're gonna play a little one on one."

Logan was inside his crease. His net sat in the middle of the ocean, and the ocean had frozen over completely. There was nothing to be seen except the light blue of frozen water.

Logan had to wait a long time, maybe even a few months.

Finally, a figure appeared on the horizon. It was a hockey player. Apparently he had a breakaway.

After a long time (maybe even a few days) the figure was close enough to be seen clearly. It was Zortron, of course. Who else would look like a gigantic praying mantis wearing a suit of hockey equipment? Zortron's blood-red jersey had SIRIUS MINDFUCKERS written on it.

Zortron kept coming with the puck. He seemed very skilled, and Logan surmised that they had some good coaching up on Sirius, probably a Canadian. It made Logan mad to think of some discontented lad from Medicine Hat going to coach on the Dogstar just because he was too short to get an NHL contract.

Logan had plenty of time for such ruminations because it was taking Zortron an awfully long time to get within shooting distance. It was taking him forever.

Logan noticed that there were people on the sidelines. To one side, many miles away, he seemed to have a small clutch of supporters. Kristal Donahue was among them. He saw also that Kristal was indecorously drunk and singing Rugby Union tunes. The strangely dressed little boy was there; so were Charlene and Lottie Luttor. Joe and Jay Fineweather were there, arms locked across each other's shoulders.

On the other side, many miles away, were people with banners that read GO, SIRIUS!! and MAKE 'EM SORRY, ZORRY!! This collection was much bigger, and included Bram Ridout, Lindy Olver, Buck Tanager (*and* Elmore Daisy), King McGee, Dr. Bermondsey, Harriet Rollins, Edna and Sam Logan, Pluto and Neptunia Logan, and Don and Dan.

Logan began to laugh. A soft wind swept across the ice.

Yahoo tapped Logan's shoulder; Logan turned and grinned.

Yahoo spoke a strange tongue, but Logan understood.

Logan nodded. "You take good care of that boy, Yahoo. Don't let him try to be like me."

Yahoo flew south. Logan was on his own. Zortron drew nearer.

To while away the time, Logan sang "Try to Remember (the Kind of September)." In his dream, Logan had a good voice. He sang the whole song and didn't spill a teardrop.

Then, instantly, Zortron was right in front of him. Zortron cocked his stick and whacked the puck. It flew at Logan. Logan decided to block the shot with his chest.

The puck hit Logan's heart and fit nicely into the hole there.

∞   ∞   ∞

The pipe had yet to be lit properly, despite all of Dr. Bermondsey's best tamping and firing procedures. "After Logan's accident," the psychiatrist contined, "I was alarmed to find him hanging about the hospital grounds once more. I told him I thought it best if he stay away, but he was not to be dissuaded. Finally, I arranged—my wife, Heloise, is Elmore Daisy's sister, you see—to have Logan come and play here for the Falcons. As long as Logan stays away from the hospital, he should be fine. But Ed Statler, owner of the Bullets, told me just the other day that he and Elmore were negotiating a trade that would send Logan back to South Grouse. The decision hinged on whether or not he won this game. I came immediately."

∞   ∞   ∞

Logan woke up. Kristal was sleeping in a chair beside his bed. Logan tried to say something, but his first attempt produced only a rough breath. He cleared his throat and managed to say, "Hi."

Kristal's eyes popped open. She smiled. "Mars, baby."

Logan took a peek at his surroundings. Hospital. He remembered the radio tower. "Joe?" he asked.

Kristal shook her head. "No Joe. Sorry, chief."

Logan began to move his limbs experimentally beneath the sheets. "I'm okay?"

"Yeah, you're okay. And you got Lindy Olver to thank for it."

"Lindy?"

"He tried to catch you."

"Where is he?" Logan was falling asleep again. He was on some pretty high-powered drugs, but his next slumber would be dreamless and deep.

"He's in surgery. Go back to sleep, Logan. I'll be here when you wake up."

∞   ∞   ∞

The Hope Blazers got on their bus and drove the seventy-five miles back to Hope. The men had jobs, families, lives in Hope. Bram Ridout didn't have a job, but his mother had told him over the telephone that the truant officer had been asking questions. As far as the Hope Blazers were concerned, the game was a tie. Only Ridout questioned the outcome. He sat at the back of the bus, scowling and playing with a stupendous pimple on his cheek. "No such a thing as a tie in the OPHL," he snarled. "Din't you jagovs ever read the friggin' rules?"

The people from "Hockey Night in Canada" left Falconbridge, too. At least, most of them did. Don and Dan, hung over and green, were somehow overlooked and left behind. Incidentally, they were scheduled to be that week's guest on "The Buck Tanager Adventure Hour."

King McGee left Falconbridge, chauffeur-driven in a Hockey Night in Canada limo. He was their New Voice. Darla Featherstone went to Toronto with King, to see if they needed a New Body.

And Logan's family went back to South Grouse, back to where the walls were soft.

Everyone thought the game ended in a tie. Later that day

Kristal Donahue mentioned to Logan that the game was understood to have ended in a tie. Logan shook his head, pronounced the outcome "unacceptable."

∞   ∞   ∞

Lindy was put in the bed beside Logan's. He was heavily sedated and slept for two days. Logan spent a long time looking at Lindy sleeping. Logan couldn't help thinking of a little boy, snow-suited and laughing in the back yard.

Lindy's sleep was troubled. Often he tried to kick out with his legs, but both his legs were wrapped in pounds of plaster, so all he managed to do was make them vibrate a little. Logan guessed that Lindy, too, was playing hockey with the Sirius mindfuckers. Logan wished him luck.

When Lindy woke up, he woke up with a small scream. Logan turned, saw that Olver was covered with sweat. Lindy breathed hard and wiped tears from his eyes. He spent a moment reclaiming his breath and staring the length of his body. The cast came up from his toes, all the way to his nipples. "Jesus," said Lindy Olver.

"Hello, Lindbergh."

Lindy turned his head. "Get a load of this, Logey!" he cried, nodding toward the body-cast. Lindy tried hard not to sound frightened. "Did I break every bone in my body or what?"

"Not every bone."

"Did I break my dick?"

"No," laughed Logan, "but what kind of Born Again thing is that to say?"

"Christ," Lindy whispered, "I forgot all about that." He tried to hold back a laugh. "Can't you see me doing that on the Christian Broadcasting Network? *I knew that Our Lord loved me because He did not allow my dick to be broken!*" Lindy laughed a strange laugh. "Logey, don't tell people I was talking like this."

"What, like a human being?"

Lindy shrugged. "Whatever."

Logan said, "They say you caught me."

"I *tried* to catch you." Lindy turned his head so that he was staring into Logan's eyes. "Logan?"

"Yeah?"

"You weigh a lot."

When Jay Fineweather and Kristal Donahue entered the room they found both men laughing.

∞   ∞   ∞

Later that afternoon, Logan received a phone call, had a short conversation.

Lindy watched him cradle the phone. "Who dat?"

"The fucking kid," answered Logan, scratching himself.

"Ridout?"

"Yo."

"What did he want?"

"Well, he didn't say for us both to get well soon."

"Naturally."

"He just phoned to say there's no such a thing as a tie in the OPHL."

"No such thing. This we knew."

Logan rolled over onto his stomach. Lindy watched with envy. Logan said, "There's not a lot we can do about it."

Lindy stared up at the ceiling. Lindy knew the ceiling by heart. He spent twenty hours a day gazing at it, looking for God. "Finish the game," said Lindy.

"Get Daisy or Tanager or whatever his name is to reschedule the game and all that shit?"

Lindy Olver thought he saw something up on the ceiling. "Shinny on the Rounder," he said quietly.

"Come again, Lindhurst?"

"Shinny on the Rounder."

Logan flipped over again. He thought he saw something up on the ceiling. "Now there's an idea."

∞   ∞   ∞

They released Logan the next day. Kristal came to get him, but she waited outside while he said goodbye to Lindy.

"I asked the doctor about it," Logan told Lindy. "He said it'd be okay, as long as you had a nurse there with you."

"Can it be Marge?"

"Lindy . . ." Logan assumed a serious tone and sat down on his friend's bed. "When you said that, there was a distinct *devilish* gleam to your eyes."

"I know, Logey. It's tough."

"Believing in God?"

"No. That's easy. It's all the other stuff that's tough. Hey. You believe in God, man?"

Logan picked up his kit and walked for the door. "Sure I do, Lindy. I'm related to him."

"See you, Logey."

"Saturday."

∞   ∞   ∞

On Saturday, Logan went to Big George Tyack's little bungalow. He knocked on the front door, received no answer. He tried again, harder, and still got no response. Something told Logan that Big George was inside. Logan twisted the knob and the front door swung open.

Though the sun outside was cruel, inside Tyack's bungalow there was a kind of Arctic twilight. Logan tried the pretty little livingroom and the dainty little kitchen; the coach was in neither. Logan checked the bathroom just in case, then he reluctantly entered the Tyack library.

Big George sat in the middle of the floor. The odd volume

still sat toppled on the shelves, but the greater part of George's book collection was spread out across the hardwood floor.

The coach hadn't slept for a very long time. His eyes looked like two coals burning in the middle of his face. George's beard had sprouted grey and sickly. Likewise grey and sickly was his general complexion. Big George would need considerable cosmetic improvement to look dead.

The coach pulled open a book and skimmed the pages wearily. He couldn't find whatever he was looking for, and he hurled the thing away angrily, missing Logan's ear by about an inch.

"Hey, Coach," said Logan merrily.

George Tyack ignored Logan, snatching up another volume and checking the index. Frustrated once more, he crumpled the book between his massive hands.

"What's happening, Coach?"

This question seemed to pierce George's consciousness. "That's what I'd like to know."

"Working on the Sirius problem?"

Big George continued to search through his books; his answer was off-hand and distracted. "The bozos."

"Bozos, huh? A bunch of clowns like?"

"Huh?" Tyack climbed to his feet and crossed to the shelves. A fat book sat on the uppermost level. Big George jumped into the air and plucked it off. "Not clowns," he said, setting the volume on the floor. "Bozos." The fat book was called *Magick in Theory & Practice*. The coach opened to the index, ran his finger up and down the columns until he found, *bozos, the*. Big George flipped pages impatiently. "They're a tribe that lives next door to the Dogons. And according to them—" George Tyack let the sentence dangle, startled by whatever his research had uncovered. "What they say is—" He stopped abruptly, ran to get another book, this one entitled *The Illuminoids*. Big George held *The Illuminoids* in one hand and cross-referenced a passage in *Magick in Theory & Practice*.

Then Big George laughed. It started off small, a giggle somewhere deep in his potbelly. The giggle bounced around inside Big George's stomach and gradually built up volume and momentum. It began to ring in his throat, whipping back and forth with more and more force until finally the laugh exploded full-blown through his mouth and nostrils. The coach stumbled backwards onto a couch and continued to laugh; it was many minutes before he was finished.

Logan grinned at him. "So what's the big joke?"

"The joke!" Tyack screamed, struggling to his feet. "The joke is—" The laugh engulfed him once more. "The joke is, Logan," he said (quietly and gingerly, because at any moment the laugh might fly him away), "the joke is that Dogstar Sirius is . . . is . . ."

Logan nodded. "Friendly. That's what I came to tell you."

"FRIENDLY!!" Big George hollered at the top of his lungs. The laugh came like a linebacker, taking on the coach's knees, slamming him into a wall. "Friendly," Tyack repeated, exhausted. "How did you find out?"

Logan shrugged. "It just came to me."

"The Bozos knew all the time. But who's gonna listen to a tribe named the Bozos?"

"I think it's a good name. I think the team should be renamed the Falconbridge Bozos."

The coach was reminded of hockey. "My oh my, wasn't that a game."

"The opera ain't over till the fat lady sings."

"Yes, I know. But I was talking about the hockey game."

"It's not over."

"Yeah, it is. A zero—zero tie."

"We're finishing the game. We're playing out on the Rounder in about an hour and a half. Which is why I came over. We don't stand a chance without our coach."

Big George tilted his head in a quizzical, dog-like manner. "Out on the river?"

"You bet."

"Shinny on the Rounder?"

"Yo."

"Oh, boy," said Big George. It seemed to make perfect sense to him. Mind you, almost everything made perfect sense to Coach George Tyack. He picked up *Magick in Theory & Practice* and tucked it gently under his arm. "Let us leave," said the coach.

Twenty-two

Once, when they were young with hearts that were whole, Logan and Lindy played shinny on the Rounder. It was Christmas Eve, but Logan's family were in the asylum and Lindy had no family at all. So they had gone to the river, on a clear and star-filled night. They took with them two bottles of Irish whiskey, they buried them up to their necks in snow.

They found the place where the moon was. This one place where the moon was, everyone else in the world saw it from an oblique angle.

The river was wide there, as wide as their hearts. At the time, both Lindy and Logan were unlucky in love, but that didn't seem to matter. The moon and the river were enough.

And on the Rounder they played shinny, a long time ago.

∞ ∞ ∞

The Falconbridge Falcons supplied the actual equipment, but all that amounted to was a bucketful of pucks and the two goal nets. The spot on Round River was just about as wide as a hockey rink, bounded on either side by high banks of snow. The Falcons judged the distance between the nets by eye and anchored them with stones and chunks of ice.

When the bus from Hope arrived (and the limousine from the hospital, depositing a wheelchair, Lindy Olver and attendant) everything was all set up, and had been for over an hour. The Falcons had amused themselves by playing a version of Tag invented by Mars Logan. In this game, one man (Mars) was designated Big Bozo. Any man he touched became a Bozo as well.

Lindy cupped his hands around his mouth and shouted, "Logey! You know I'm still rooting for Hope, don't you?"

The two coaches met in the middle of the river and tossed a coin. George Tyack called it Horace by which he meant Horus by which he meant heads. Horace it was. George chose the net that lay to the east.

Logan skated to his appointed keep. Near it was an old dead tree. As he approached, it seemed to Logan that the tree spoke. "Greetings and salutations!"

Logan was in such a good mood that a talking tree didn't really faze him; he checked the branches only because the voice seemed somehow familiar. Grinning high in the air was the strangely dressed little boy.

"Hey, But! How in the world did you get up there?"

"Interpolation of topology and applied physics."

"Do tell."

"I climbed."

"How did you know we were going to be here?"

"Your wife informed me."

"My wife?"

"The young woman standing over there."

"Oh," mumbled Logan, "she ain't my wife."

Little Anthony looked perplexed. "Nay?"

"Nay," repeated Logan with a chuckle, batting chunks of ice down the ice.

"I referred to her as Mrs. Logan, yet she made no protest. Could it be she is laboured with a hearing impediment?"

"I guess that's what it is."

"Here comes the face-off!" pointed Anthony O'Toole.

Logan fitted the mask over his face, the one that showed a flying eagle slicing through clouds.

Logan assumed his stance.

∞   ∞   ∞

One of the highlights of the afternoon occurred when Bram Ridout made a one-man rush the length of the ice. He stopped a puck and, instead of flipping it into free territory, started coming with it. There were no lines painted on the river, after all, something that would have greatly pleased the late Joe Fineweather. Ridout started coming, and the players from both teams went to the side to cheer him on. Lindy Olver tried to stand up and immediately keeled over. Even Logan muttered, "Go, kid, go." Ridout skated so quickly that his three-eyed lightning-filled mask slipped from his head. The boy's face was blushing red, covered with sweat. Logan was suddenly alarmed by Ridout's youth. Bram grinned and bit the tip of his tongue. When he got within ten feet of Logan he reared back with his stick and attempted to whack the puck. He fanned on it, and the momentum of his swing tossed him head-first onto the ice. Ridout crashed into Logan, knocking him down as well.

Logan took Ridout's head into the crook of his arm and administered the playful (but painful) knuckles to the head.

That play was recorded by Ms. Mickey Moonie, now employed, thanks to her ability at gathering scoops, by the Falconbridge *Morning Star*. She stood alone, isolated. She juggled two bottles of Remy Martin and a cigarette, a pen, and her stenopad. Somehow she managed to record everything that was happening on the Rounder.

Mickey Moonie wasn't the only spectator. Kristal Donahue was there, wearing a Falconbridge Falcons jersey. Lottie Luttor was there, hand-in-hand with daughter Charlene. Buck Tanager was there. A matronly woman in a leopard-skin coat, who every three or four seconds would look up into the tree's branches, anxious about the strangely dressed little boy, was there.

The next note Mickey Moonie of the *Morning Star* made was to the effect that the coach of the Falcons (G. Tyack) inserted himself into the line-up. Big George came tumbling onto the ice in a pair of borrowed skates, installing himself at right defence. Immediately he showed evidence of his championship style. Lars Løkan smashed a heavy slapshot toward Logan's net. Big George threw himself sideways. There was a loud, mushy *toink* as the puck bounced from his head.

Logan rushed quickly to the coach's side. "Are you okay?"

"Sure, I'm okay," said the coach, lumbering upwards. "Why wouldn't I be okay?"

The other thing George did reminiscent of his playing days was to deliver a stunning open-ice bodycheck against the person of Løkan, Kizzle fakir. The check was so stunning as to lift the massive Lars into the air (where he did an awkward but recognizable triple half-gainer) and to land him head-first in a deep pile of snow.

Because Big George Tyack was playing the game, he had to appoint a new coach for the afternoon. The new coach was completely hidden behind a snowdrift. He had been named by Big George because of his extensive knowledge and wisdom of the I Ching. The new coach was tossing the coins at a dizzying clip. Luk Sun Li was very excited. Logan knew this when the ancient Chinese dwarf climbed on top of the drift and shouted something so strange that he immediately disappeared.

They played and laughed on the Rounder. Everyone played with their whole hearts, and everyone played as well as they ever would. No one scored.

They played until the sun began to sink beneath the earth.

The sun was in Logan's eyes. Now, as he watched, the players became dark forms surrounded by light. They looked like shadows and they looked like angels.

One Hope player began to shine brighter than the rest. Logan couldn't tell which one it was.

Logan watched the man come down the ice.   •

It was the instant before the day gave way to the winter's dark night.

When the Hope man shot, the puck became lost in the last piece of the sun.

Logan fell to the ice. Logan tried to burst out of his body so that he could cover all of the net. Logan felt something tap his right shoulder.

Then the night fell.

∞   ∞   ∞

The Falcons lined up against the bus from Hope so that they could shake hands with the Blazers as they boarded.

All of the Blazers were very complimentary to Logan. "You were just great, man. It's a damn shame someone had to lose the game."

Logan shrugged.

Bram Ridout approached, proferring a pale and slender hand. "Good game, Logan."

"Fucking kid."

A strange look covered Bram's mottled face. It was half cocky, half coy. "Hey, Logan. The other night, just before the power went in the arena, guess what?"

"What?"

"That puck was by me, man."

Logan nodded. "I figured."

"So, in a sense, you won. But I'm the only guy who knows, and you're the only one I'm telling." Bram managed to contain a chuckle. "Hard lines, journeyman."

"It was a good game," judged Logan.

"Yeah. But you should work on your style. You go down too easy. You got lucky so many times it made me sick."

"I'll work on it."

"Sorry about that crack I made. Fifteen dog turds for a Logan pudding coin."

"Forget it."

Ridout leant closer. " 'Cause I'll tell you, you couldn't trade a Logan coin for nothing."

"Get on the bus."

The engine was started and the bus moved away, toward Hope.

∞   ∞   ∞

Charlene Luttor came racing up to Logan. "I found one, I found one!" Charlene was very excited and couldn't stand still. She hugged Logan briefly and then was off again in circles. "It was there, just like you said!"

"What, Charlene?"

"A consolation! Up in the sky!" Charlene grabbed his hand and pulled him away. "I'll show you."

A small hill was crested in the moonlight. The two stood on top, alone in the night.

"Now, look!" commanded Charlene, pointing into the starfields. "There's his head. And he's got a bow and arrow."

Logan squinted and stared into darkness. "I can't really make it out, Charlene."

"You're not trying! It's a consolation. There's his head." She waved at the stars. "He's a hunter."

Logan looked again and tried as hard as he could.

"Hey!" cried the girl. "He's got a dog with him!" Apparently Charlene hadn't noticed this before. "Can you see the dog?"

Logan shook his head mournfully.

Charlene made her hands into tiny fists and placed them sternly to her sides. "This is very simple. I'm going to show you. Okay?"

"Yeah, show me."

"Now, you see that star there? The one that's brighter than all the rest?"

One star caught Logan's attention; it did appear to be brighter than all the other stars in the sky.

Indeed, it is about three hundred times brighter than the average sixth magnitude star. It is also the nearest star, at a distance of 8.7 light years. For these reasons, it is the most visible in the nightscape.

"Yeah! I see it."

"That's part of the dog," explained Charlene patiently. "And beside it, over there, is the hunter man. It's easy."

Logan closed his eyes and did something that resembled prayer. He took Charlene's hand and held it tightly, nervously. Then Logan opened his eyes.

Logan saw Orion and the Greater Dog. "Yahoo!" he bellowed. Logan spun around. "And look, Charlene! Look over there! A bull!"

The little girl followed Logan's gaze. "Yup. That's a bull, okay."

In a matter of moments they had also located a unicorn and a rabbit. Then Logan took Charlene's hand and they went back down the hill.

And, in case anyone asks you what you learned today, tell them this: the brightest star in the sky is the Dogstar Sirius.